Trust

Sage Gardens Cozy Mystery Series

Cindy Bell

Copyright © 2015 Cindy Bell

All rights reserved.

All rights reserved. No part of this publication may be reproduced or transmitted in any form or by any means, electronic or mechanical, including photocopy, recording, or any information storage or retrieval system, without permission in writing from the publisher.

This is a work of fiction. The characters, incidents and locations portrayed in this book and the names herein are fictitious. Any similarity to or identification with the locations, names, characters or history of any person, product or entity is entirely coincidental and unintentional.

All trademarks and brands referred to in this book are for illustrative purposes only, are the property of their respective owners and not affiliated with this publication in any way. Any trademarks are being used without permission, and the publication of the trademark is not authorized by, associated with or sponsored by the trademark owner.

ISBN-13: 978-1512276541

ISBN-10: 1512276545

Table of Contents

Chapter One

Morning in Sage Gardens was usually a peaceful time, filled with tweeting birds and cheerful residents waving to one another. In such a beautiful environment it was easy to be eager to greet the day. Although many of the people who lived in Sage Gardens were early risers they took care not to disturb those that weren't. Lawnmowers, radios, and loud noise in general were kept for after a reasonable hour.

When the blaring siren of a police car shattered the comfortable silence of a community awakening, it was a surprise. It had knocked Eddy right out of his half-asleep half-awake state. Out of habit Eddy launched out of his bed ready to deal with whatever crime was taking place. It was only as he pulled on his shoes and a t-shirt that he recalled he was no longer an active police officer. Still the sirens drew him out the door of his villa and onto the lush, green grass of his front lawn.

As Eddy reached the walkway a police car blazed right past him. Eddy's heart pounded as he looked in the direction that the car was travelling. Its flashing lights and blaring siren were so out of place amidst the pink flamingos and garden gnomes that decorated the front yards of the villas. He wondered what might have happened. It was clear that whatever it was had to be quite serious.

With his attention sharpened by the sights and sounds Eddy watched as another police car blew through the entrance of Sage Gardens. Despite his concern for what had happened, he felt a rush of adrenaline flood him. He smiled as every nerve in his body stood on edge, prepared to protect or attack as needed.

When Eddy was a policeman every single time he went out on a call and got to flip on the lights and the siren, his entire body would react to the urgency of the situation. It wasn't exactly a thrill, as many times the situation that he was racing towards was dire, but it did make his adrenaline pump because he had to be prepared for anything. He still got that feeling, even forty years later.

Eddy watched as the car raced up the hill to the villas that overlooked the distant highway. He knew a few of the residents that lived in that area. He could see that an ambulance and a police car were already parked on the hill. Eddy presumed that they must have approached earlier from the other side of Sage Gardens as he hadn't heard their sirens.

Eddy was thinking about what might have occurred. His thoughts were soon distracted by the sound of wheels against the sidewalk. He turned around with a smile as he knew it would be Abe. Abe was one of the few residents that was both in a wheelchair and yet still active. Some of the wheelchair-bound residents spent more time in their villa and only emerged for trips or transport to a doctor's appointment.

Abe was one of the 'rollers' who was always

out and about, which made it very easy to recognize the sound of his wheelchair. Abe was a younger resident compared to many. His short, brown hair didn't have a trace of gray. His light, brown eyes had yet to gain any wrinkles around them. He normally looked fairly healthy, but Eddy noticed something off about him right away.

"How are you, Abe?" Eddy squinted at the man who seemed much paler than usual. His expression was grave. "Are you ill?"

"No, I'm fine. But Joel Westons isn't." Abe grimaced and looked over his shoulder up at the hill where the police cars had come to a stop.

"Joel?" Eddy frowned. The name was familiar, as just about everyone knew everyone in Sage Gardens, but he couldn't place a face to it. "Is that what the police and ambulance are here for?"

"I thought someone would have told you before I had the chance to, news travels so fast around here," Abe lowered his voice to a conspiratorial tone. "Joel's wife, Anna, found him dead on the living room floor this morning." His eyes widened as he revealed the news. Eddy's did as well.

"Dead?" Eddy shook his head with a frown. It wasn't that unusual for residents to suddenly pass from medical conditions. But deaths of that kind, were rarely attended to by several patrol cars full of policemen. "I guess it wasn't natural causes?"

"Not unless there's a way to naturally get your head bashed in," Abe replied gruffly. He coughed sharply once, and then shook his head. "Someone did him in with a candlestick."

"Must have been a heavy one?" Eddy turned to look as another police car shot by them both. The siren made conversation impossible for a moment.

"Must have been. I can't believe he's dead," Abe said grimly.

"Did you know him well?"

"He and I would get together now and then for lunch. His wife volunteers at the local library, so he's often alone during the day." Abe sighed and rolled his chair back a few inches to get a better view of the hill. "It's a damn shame that he's gone. He was a decent guy, you know? I hope they figure out who did this." He lowered his voice with disgust, "In his own home."

Eddy's attention was focused on the crime the moment he discovered that it was a murder. He had worked as a homicide detective and had proved himself a vicious interrogator with good instincts over the years. He had worked many homicides and he knew that a bludgeoning death was one of the rarest, especially in home invasions. It was intriguing to him to think of, but that wasn't the only reason that he was interested. Eddy had a strong protective instinct, and any crime that took place in his neighborhood felt like a personal attack.

"Do they have any suspects in mind?" Eddy's interest was piqued at the idea of a new case to look into. He had begun to settle into his role as resident detective. Most of his neighbors were used to it as well.

"Not that I know of just yet, I mean he wasn't found very long ago. But maybe you could find out more than I can." Abe lifted an eyebrow. Eddy realized that Abe wasn't just being friendly, he wanted information. Eddy understood why. It was hard to discover that a friend had passed, it was harder when the loss was the result of a murder.

"I'll see what I can find out." Eddy clapped his hand lightly on Abe's shoulder. "I'm sorry for your loss, Abe."

"Thanks." Abe looked up the hill in the direction of Joel's villa. "I don't know what happened, Eddy, but I do know he didn't deserve this. Neither did Anna."

"I'm sure that they didn't." Eddy tightened his lips. Murder was the type of crime that could tear apart not just a family, but an entire community. Though he had become accustomed to it over the years, it was always disturbing to him.

As Eddy ascended the hill in the direction of

the Westons' villa, he ignored the subtle aches in his hip and lower back. He was determined to stay in shape as he neared seventy, but it was a lot more difficult to accomplish that than it had been when he was twenty. His eating habits didn't exactly help either.

When he reached the crest of the hill he could see several police cars, as well as the coroner's van. He frowned and began to approach the villa. Before he could get too close, he noticed someone walking towards it from another direction. The woman was moving with a sense of determination that always made Eddy feel just a little tired, as if he was already exhausted by the fight that he expected to have. Her coppery hair was tightly braided as usual, but a few flyaway strands were being bullied by the light breeze. Even from a distance he could see her frowning.

"Samantha, of course," he muttered and shook his head. He couldn't help but feel a twinge of admiration for the woman. She was as determined as she was intelligent and she always had her nose in any kind of mystery. She also happened to be one of the few good friends he had made since moving to Sage Gardens. She smiled when she spotted him. Her smile transformed her from a force to be reckoned with to a friendly soul.

"Eddy!" She waved to him and immediately shifted direction to walk towards him. Eddy paused to wait for her.

"I heard all of the sirens," Samantha explained as she reached his side. She offered a worried frown. "It's not good news is it?"

"I'm afraid not." Eddy looked past her as a stretcher was rolled out of the house with a body bag on it. "Joel Westons from what I understand."

"Poor man." Samantha shook her head with genuine grief in her bright green eyes. "He and Anna were one of the sweetest couples I ever met."

"You knew them well?" Eddy asked with some surprise. He had never heard Samantha mention them before.

"Not especially well. We shared a game of cards now and then with a few others. Not lately though." She shook her head again as the doors of the coroner's van slammed shut. "I guess I should have checked in on them."

"No way anyone could have known, I'm sure. A friend of Joel's, Abe, asked me to see if I can find out anything about it." He gave a sidelong look in Samantha's direction. "I'm assuming that you're here to do the same?"

Samantha struggled not to smile. It wasn't appropriate to be smiling at a time of grief, but she couldn't help it. She loved having the chance to work with Eddy on a mystery. It made her feel like it was the old days when she would stock up on junk food and go on stakeouts to get to the bottom of a crime she was writing an article about. Although Eddy was a retired cop, and she was a retired crime journalist, their paths had actually been fairly similar.

"Maybe." She managed to reply without breaking out into a smile. "You forgot your hat."

He reached up and swept his hand back through his thinning, brown hair. He usually put on his fedora. If anyone asked it was because he was used to wearing it. But the truth was he was a little annoyed with the bald spots that were forming.

"I rushed out to see what was going on." He swept his gaze over her simple pants suit which looked perfect. "I guess you were already awake for the day."

"Awake? I already had breakfast, fed the ducks, walked by the water and…"

"Okay, enough." Eddy felt that exhaustion kick in. Samantha had far too much energy for him.

Samantha smiled at the weariness in Eddy's dark blue eyes. She had decided not long after they met that it was going to be her duty to teach the far too serious man to lighten up and enjoy life. So far he wasn't the most willing student.

"I'm sorry. I am very curious about what

happened to Joel. I hope they investigate it thoroughly even though Joel was elderly," she stated.

"I'm sure they will, Samantha. Police treat every crime with the same respect," Eddy said sternly. He and Samantha often argued when it came to the role of police in the community and their behavior. While Eddy knew that some cops weren't the most honest, he also knew just how much of their lives they invested in what others considered just a job.

"Fine, if that's the case then there should be no need for us to investigate." Samantha smiled sweetly. Eddy narrowed his eyes. He knew that she had him there. He wasn't about to stand by and wait for an investigation to take place. He wanted to get to the bottom of it just as much as Samantha did. He wanted Sage Gardens to feel safe again.

"It doesn't hurt to have a few extra pairs of eyes on the situation. I'll see what there is to know. You keep an eye out for anyone acting suspiciously." He began to walk towards the villa. It was already blocked off with crime tape and cones. He ignored the yellow crime tape and walked right up to the nearest police officer. The officer looked up at him with a hint of recognition, as if he knew Eddy's face, but not his name.

Eddy still kept in contact with some associates in the police department, and his reputation was well-known.

"What's the situation?" Eddy's tone implied that he deserved to know every detail.

"The situation is that a crime has taken place, and unless you're a police officer I don't have anything to say to you." The officer narrowed his eyes.

"There's no need to play tough guy. I'm not asking for your badge, I just want to know what happened here." Eddy narrowed his eyes right back. "I think if you check with your supervisor she would be fine with you sharing a few details. But then you'd have to explain why you didn't show a retired homicide detective more respect."

"Oh, well I…" The officer looked down at his polished shoes for a moment and then back up at Eddy. "All right, but I can only tell you so much."

"Whatever you're comfortable with." Eddy smiled at him charmingly.

"Looks like someone climbed in through an open window and bludgeoned the victim from behind with a candlestick. According to the medical examiner it looks like it happened between nine-thirty and eleven last night. The wife found him on the floor when she woke up." He leaned a little closer to Eddy. "It must have been horrific for her to see. It was a vicious murder."

Eddy frowned. "How vicious could it have been? She didn't find him until she woke up? Wouldn't the commotion have woken her up?"

"She said that she is a bit hard of hearing and she didn't hear a thing." He sighed. "It's possible I guess if the victim was knocked out by the first blow. Or maybe she is a deep sleeper. No one expects their spouse to be murdered while they sleep. Poor thing, she's really shaken up." He nodded his head towards the woman who was huddled near an ambulance. Anna was a petite woman with delicate features. She looked to be in her fifties, but was likely pushing seventy. Her dark brown hair was cut just below her ears. She reminded Eddy of one of his favorite teachers at school and immediately he felt sympathy for her.

Anna just seemed too fragile to be dealing with such a difficult situation. Two EMTs were speaking to her. She had a blanket draped over her shoulders. From her ruffled hair it looked as if she had just gotten out of bed. Eddy could see the blood on her hands. She must have tried to revive her husband. Not only had Joel been killed, but he had been dead in his living room for several hours. To Eddy it was a dreadful thought that a death could go unnoticed for so long.

"Any suspects yet?" Eddy looked back at the officer.

"Not that I can say." The officer tightened his lips with determination. "You know I could get in trouble just for telling you this much."

"I appreciate the information." Eddy nodded and patted the officer on the back. "You're doing a great job here. I'm sure you'll do a very thorough investigation."

"I will, Sir." The officer turned and walked back towards the villa. Eddy turned towards Samantha just in time to see her walking into the yard of the neighboring villa.

"What is she up to?" he muttered so as not to draw the attention of the police officers. He was sure that whatever Samantha was doing had something to do with the investigation.

Chapter Two

Samantha picked her way carefully across the grass. She knew how hard the gardener worked to keep the grass green and lush and so she did her best to avoid trampling it. But she had spotted someone poking their head out from behind the villa and she wanted a closer look at who it was. As soon as she had begun walking towards it, the person ducked behind the villa. Samantha thought this was very suspicious. She crept closer.

Samantha noticed the person peering around the corner of the villa. She didn't recognize him right away, but his face did seem familiar. Slowly she crept closer to the villa. She had read enough crime novels to know that a murderer almost always returns to the scene of the crime. This man seemed to be very interested in remaining hidden, while still keeping an eye on what was unfolding next door.

"Hello there!" Samantha called out. She wanted others to hear her, so that they knew where she was. She wasn't about to become any murderer's victim. She heard footsteps falling behind her. The man who had been peeking around the side of the villa reluctantly stepped out from behind it. He looked annoyed as he greeted Samantha.

"Hello."

Samantha looked over her shoulder in time to see Eddy walking towards her. She knew that he would want to share the details of the case with her.

"Are you a friend of the Westons?" Samantha asked. Then suddenly she realized who it was. "Tommy, I'm sorry I didn't even recognize you."

"I got a haircut," he muttered and ran his hand lightly over his closely cropped hair.

Tommy was known around Sage Gardens for his long, stringy hair. Many of the older folk addressed him as Hippie rather than Tommy, while some just complained about the way it made the neighborhood look. Tommy had always been determined not to cut his hair. Samantha was a little surprised that he had, and how much it changed how he looked. Tommy was a fairly large man with a little weight covering up his muscular frame. With his long hair he had seemed harmless, but now with his short haircut it was as if Samantha could now see his broad frame clearly.

"Tommy." Eddy nodded to the man as he stepped up beside Samantha. "Did you hear about what happened?"

"Yes." Tommy nodded. "How could I not?" he grumbled. "I was trying to sleep when all of these sirens started blaring."

Samantha raised an eyebrow. She was surprised that Tommy, who was Joel and Anna's neighbor would be less concerned about their wellbeing and more concerned about his sleep being interrupted.

"Well, Joel's dead, Tommy," Eddy spoke flatly. Samantha knew this trick. He wanted to see how Tommy would react when he first actually heard the news.

"And?" Tommy shrugged. "I already know that. I'd have to be blind not to see the coroner's van. But if the man is dead already what's with all the sirens? It's not like getting here any faster is going to save him. Is it?" He sneered. "I think there should be a rule about coming through here with sirens on. We all know what an ambulance showing up means. Someone is dead. If it's not an emergency, then why all of the noise?"

"Have you spoken to the police yet, Tommy?" Samantha asked. She did her best not to comment on what she thought about his view of things. It seemed rather cold to her for him to be so put off by the noise.

"I have," he said with exasperation. "Not that they are going to do anything about it. What do they care? It's just another dead guy. He's not important enough for anyone to cause a fuss over."

Samantha couldn't hold back any longer. The way he was speaking about Joel made her sick to her stomach. "I'm sure his grieving wife would argue that point," she spoke through gritted teeth. In the next moment she felt Eddy's hand rest lightly on her shoulder. She knew it was more about restraining her than comforting her. Eddy had seen her temper flare before.

"Oh Anna?" Tommy snorted. "I'm sure she's not too broken up about the whole thing."

"How can you say that?" Eddy asked incredulously. "She found her husband dead in a pool of his own blood."

"Well sure, there are prettier ways to go, but she's probably just glad that he's gone. From the amount of fighting those two do, you'd think that they were enemies, not husband and wife." He brushed his hand back over his hair yet again. "Glad I dodged that bullet. Never been married, never had kids, never had a problem in my life."

Samantha pursed her lips. She reminded herself that she would get more information with honey than with venom. "Were they fighting last night, Tommy?"

"I wouldn't know. I wasn't here." He shrugged.

"Where were you?" Eddy pressed.

"I don't see how that is any of your business." Tommy crossed his arms and settled his gaze on Eddy. "Playing detective again, Eddy?"

"I was just curious," Eddy commented. "So, you didn't hear any kind of commotion when the murder took place?"

"Like I said, I wasn't here," Tommy growled. "I don't need to be grilled by the likes of you, Eddy. If you harass me in any way I'll get you arrested faster than you can even think of a question."

Eddy narrowed his eyes. "You know it's only people who have something to hide that don't cooperate."

"No, it's people that know the difference between a real cop, and an old man who misses his badge," Tommy said angrily. "You've got no right to even be on my property right now, Eddy. So, why don't you and your nosy little girlfriend shove off?"

Samantha was so furious by the end of his tirade that Eddy's squeezing hand on her shoulder did nothing to calm her. "Listen to me, Tommy Radner, if you're going to speak to Eddy or me that way you're going to face some serious consequences. This is not how you behave when your neighbor has been murdered."

"Oh, what are you going to do, Samantha?" he spat out her name. "Are you going to write an article in the Sage Gardens' weekly gazette? Oh no, that's right. You can't even get a job writing for the neighborhood gossip rag, can you?" He stared at her with open hostility. "Get off my property."

"Technically, it's not your property." Samantha looked over towards the voice and saw Walt standing a few feet from them. "No one owns their homes here. They all belong to Sage Gardens.

So, you can't really claim it as your property."

"Oh, stay out of it, Walt." Tommy waved his hand in Walt's direction and then stalked off into his villa.

Samantha shrugged Eddy's hand off her shoulder. "Why did you let him talk to you that way?" she asked more out of confusion than anger.

"Listen, Samantha it's not going to do anybody any good if Tommy and I come to blows, now is it?" Eddy shook his head. He looked towards the window of Tommy's villa just in time to see him snap the shade shut. "He certainly is acting suspicious. He seems so angry with us, he's never spoken to me that way before. Maybe he is just upset by the murder, but I think our first step should be to look into where he was last night."

"First step?" Walt looked interested. "What have I missed? Are you looking into Joel's death?"

"I think we should." Samantha glared in the

direction of Tommy's villa. "If only to make sure Tommy doesn't get away with it."

"So, you think Tommy is good for it?" Walt asked. "That's a pretty big accusation."

Samantha crossed her arms. "The last time I played cards with the Westons they had a problem with Tommy. He didn't like the way they had parked their car, and claimed it was blocking his view of the water. So, he pounded on the door until Joel came out. They squabbled a bit and then Joel just did what he asked. Apparently, that wasn't the first issue that they've had with him. It appears that Tommy is not the nicest neighbor around."

"Maybe not, but that doesn't make him a murderer." Eddy frowned. "Still, he does seem very unaffected by the whole thing."

"We should check and see if his alibi holds water," Walt suggested. "Can you get any information out of the officers, Eddy?"

"I can try," Eddy said. Samantha and Walt

lingered near the street as Eddy walked back towards the crime scene.

"What can you tell me about the neighbor?" Eddy asked. The young officer continued to roll up the yellow tape.

"Nothing."

"Oh really? Not even his alibi?" Eddy's tone became harder. "Do you think you could just let me know where he was claiming to be last night?"

"You could ask him." The officer finished rolling up the tape. "I'm not going to get in trouble over this."

"You don't have to worry about that. I'm just asking a question." Eddy met his eyes. "It's not going to do any harm to let me know where he was."

The officer frowned. He looked as if he really didn't want to share the information. Eddy raised an eyebrow.

"At the movies, okay? That's all I can tell you." He turned and walked away from Eddy with swift strides. Eddy watched him for a moment. He was a little sketchy in Eddy's opinion. It was one thing to willingly share information, and another to flat out refuse to give it. The officer that Eddy had just spoken to did neither of those things. Instead, he allowed his mind to be swayed by Eddy. That could be dangerous when wearing a uniform. As Eddy walked back towards Walt and Samantha his mind pushed and pulled at Tommy's alibi.

Samantha watched Eddy interact with the young officer. She could see that he was trying to intimidate the officer with the way he straightened his shoulders and leaned close. She had seen him do this a few times before. Walt's voice drew her from her observations.

"What do you think, Samantha?" Walt asked.

"I'm not sure. Joel always seemed like a nice guy to me. He and his wife certainly never had trouble with money." She looked over at Anna again. "Poor Anna. I don't know how she's going to handle all of this."

"It must be difficult when you prefer to be part of a couple. My wife and I always had our own space during our marriage. I've never really enjoyed living with other people." He straightened the lapel of his suit jacket.

Samantha glanced over at him quizzically. "That's not surprising."

"What is that supposed to mean?" Walt asked.

"I just mean that you seem very particular so it would be difficult for you to tolerate someone always moving things around and getting things dirty." She shook her head. "I can't see you enjoying that."

"Well, I do have my ways." Walt frowned. "Maybe I'm a little too set in them. Once in a while I wonder what it would be like to shake things up a bit."

"Really?" Samantha looked at him with genuine surprise. Before she could ask him more about that, Eddy interrupted their conversation.

"So, it turns out that Tommy's alibi is that he was at the movies. That's a pretty thin alibi. Even if he actually went to the movies, he could have slipped out once it started."

"Hmm, I don't know." Walt tapped his chin lightly. "The movie theater is at least thirty minutes away. By the time he slipped out of the theater, and drove back here, committed the murder, and then drove back, the movie would have likely been over. That would be a tight schedule to keep."

"That doesn't even take traffic into account." Samantha seemed to be doing calculations in her mind. "It would add at least ten minutes on to travel time if there was traffic. Maybe we could question someone at the theater to see if they can confirm Tommy's presence there last night."

"We could," Eddy agreed. "But I'm not sure they would remember. Hundreds of people go in and out of that movie theater every day."

"It's worth a shot." Samantha glanced over

her shoulder at Tommy's house. "I doubt he's going to be willing to tell us whether he has a ticket stub or not."

"I can check," Walt offered with a slight smile. "I'd like to get a glimpse of the inside of his villa anyway."

"Good idea." Eddy nodded. "He's going to bristle at Samantha or me asking questions."

Samantha looked over at Anna. She clutched the blanket tightly around her shoulders. She certainly looked traumatized to Samantha, but what struck her was the lack of tears. She knew that sometimes the sight of something tragic could be so shocking that a person was rendered emotionless, but she still wondered.

"I'm going to go speak to Anna."

"Are you sure?" Eddy asked. "She might be a little too raw right now."

"Let her go," Walt advised. "If anyone can handle a delicate situation, it's Sam."

"Thanks, Walt." Samantha smiled briefly at

him. Eddy scowled as if he might have more to say, but he kept it to himself. Samantha walked towards Anna who was still near the ambulance. It appeared that the medics had cleared her, however she still seemed shaken.

"Anna." Samantha reached a hand out to her. "I'm so sorry for your loss." Anna stared at her for a moment, as if she didn't quite recognize her, then slowly it registered in her expression.

"Thank you, Samantha," she spoke quietly, but her voice did not tremble. Samantha took Anna's hand in her own. She noticed that the woman's hands were not shaking, but they were a little sweaty. In her years of trying to gather as much information as possible she had learned a trick or two to know whether someone was telling the truth or not. Sweaty hands almost always indicated deceit. However, in this situation they didn't really reveal much. With the stress of what Anna had seen, and the sudden loss of her husband there could have been numerous reasons for her sweaty palms.

"Is there anything you need? Anyone I can call for you?" Samantha offered.

"No, I don't need anything." Anna pressed a balled up tissue against her nose.

"I'm sorry again, Anna. I hope you know that I'm here to help if you need it." Samantha gave her hand a slight squeeze, then let go of it.

"Thank you, Samantha. I don't even know what to think right now. I went to bed last night happy, and woke up this morning a widow. It's such a hard thing to wrap my head around." She sighed. "Joel is gone."

Her words sounded mournful, but her expression was still rather indifferent. Samantha noticed that Anna didn't even cringe when she spoke of her husband being dead, or her being a widow.

"Do you have any idea who might have done this?" Samantha asked. Anna looked over at her with narrowed eyes.

"Of course not. How would I know? Joel

barely spoke to me anymore. I didn't know what he was doing when I wasn't home, and I didn't care to. We had let things get pretty distant between us." She tightened the blanket around her shoulders. "I guess that makes this easier."

Samantha nodded. She wasn't sure how it could make anything easier, but she wasn't going to argue with Anna. "Are you sure there isn't someone I could call? One of your children maybe?"

"We didn't have any. I had a son with my first husband, but he has nothing to do with me. Joel and I never wanted to have kids." She pressed her lips together briefly as if trying to suppress a rising emotion. "I guess that was for the best."

Samantha couldn't imagine love becoming so unemotional. But then she had witnessed plenty of marriages that didn't involve love. Sometimes marriage just seemed like the right thing to do at the time, or perhaps it was a matter of settling. Her own marriage, though very brief, had been passionate and overwhelming. She still thought about her ex-husband at times, even though it had been so many years. She couldn't imagine feeling nothing at all for him.

"Anna, if you think of any way that I can help, please feel free to call me." Samantha looked into the woman's eyes. "No one should be alone at a time like this."

"Maybe not." Anna looked solemnly towards the house. "But that's where I am. Thanks Samantha, but I have some things to take care of now."

"Of course." Samantha watched as Anna trudged slowly back towards the house.

Chapter Three

Eddy continued to observe the police officers and their processing of the crime scene as Walt walked up to Tommy's villa. He knocked on the door with three firm knocks. It was the same knock he had been using for many years. He felt it got the job done well, with getting the attention of the person inside, making it clear that it was important, and that he was not going to go away. After a moment the door jerked open. Tommy stuck his face out with a grim frown. "What do you want?"

"I just wanted to ask you a quick question." Walt studied the man intently. He immediately noticed how uneven his hair was cut. It was short, but it was not cut to one length. To Walt it looked more like someone had taken a lawnmower to the man's head.

"Why would I answer any question from you?" Tommy glowered at him.

"Oh, it's not about all of that." Walt waved his hand dismissively in the direction of the crime scene. "I saw you last night at the movie theater. I have this deal with a friend of mine that if I have more movie ticket stubs than him, he has to pay for dinner the next time our film club gets together. Now, I know that I'll have more than him, or rather I would have if I hadn't thrown out my ticket stub accidentally with my popcorn. I was wondering if you had yours? I could even give you a dollar or two for it." Walt began to reach into his pocket for his wallet.

"You didn't see me last night," Tommy's voice was gruff.

"Weren't you at the movies?" Walt feigned innocence. "Maybe I had you mixed up with someone else?"

"I was at the movies. But you didn't see me." Tommy glared at him.

"Okay, if you say so. Either way, do you happen to have your ticket stub?" Walt smiled.

"No, I don't. I threw it out. No one keeps those except for teenage girls and weirdos. Is that what you are? A weirdo?" Tommy raised an eyebrow and offered a menacing expression. Walt was more than a little intimidated. He wasn't expecting Tommy to be so aggressive. His anxiety began rising very quickly.

"No, I am not that at all. I just asked a simple question." Walt cleared his throat. "I'm not sure where you've learned your manners from, but you are quite rude."

"I've had a rough morning." Tommy forced a smile and then snapped the door closed. Walt was a little dazed by Tommy's abruptness. He didn't often attempt to socialize with others, as he preferred a book to company most of the time. As he walked back towards Eddy he felt as if he had just had that habit reinforced. Samantha was walking back towards Eddy at the same time. Eddy noticed her troubled expression.

"Are you okay?" Eddy studied her.

"I just think it's so sad." Samantha shook her head. No matter how many stories she had worked on in the past she had never mastered the ability to be emotionally distant from the tragedies and crimes she learned about. "She doesn't even seem like she is going to miss him."

Eddy raised an eyebrow. "Trust me, my ex-wife wouldn't have missed me."

Samantha looked at him with some sympathy. "That must hurt."

"Not at all. I wouldn't miss her either." Eddy chuckled. "Some people are better off having never known each other. Don't you think? Your marriage wasn't exactly stellar either, was it?" He looked at her curiously.

Samantha narrowed her eyes. "No, I guess it wasn't, but I would absolutely miss my ex-husband if he were to die. I would even attend his funeral if someone thought to inform me."

"That's very tender of you, Sam." Walt smiled warmly at her.

"Just because things didn't work out doesn't mean that I stopped loving him." Samantha glanced wistfully away, but then pulled her thoughts back to the moment. "But that has nothing to do with any of this. We need to be focused on this crime, because I have a feeling it's not going to be very simple to solve. At this time I'm not even willing to rule out Anna as a suspect."

"Good point. How could she have slept through her husband being killed in that way? I'm not buying it." Eddy looked sternly in the direction of the house.

"Really? You think Anna is a suspect?" Walt looked between them incredulously. "Did either of you notice her size?"

"She is quite petite." Samantha considered the difference in Joel's size and Anna's. "But Joel wasn't a big man either. Besides, he was hit from behind. Anyone can overpower someone if they're not expecting an attack."

"That's true," Eddy agreed. "She doesn't exactly have an alibi for the time of the murder. Still, what motivation could she have had for killing him?"

"Money, it's always money," Walt stated with conviction.

"Not always." Samantha looked back towards the villa. "Sometimes it can be about passion."

"Wait just a minute. Don't you think if Anna had been the one to strike him that hard, she would have gotten blood on her face, clothing, even her hair?" Walt shuddered at the thought. "Do you really think she could have hidden all of that?"

Eddy's eyes grew wide.

"What is it?" Samantha asked when she noticed his expression.

"Tommy had a haircut." Eddy stared at Tommy's villa. "A very short haircut."

"You're right," Samantha replied slowly. "If he was the one who attacked Joel, maybe he panicked and got his hair cut to hide the evidence."

"Wouldn't a barber notice that though?" Eddy queried.

"A barber didn't cut that man's hair." Walt pursed his lips. "I've never seen a more uneven haircut. I am pretty sure that he did that to himself."

"That makes more sense." Samantha noticed a few of the officers leaving Joel's villa. One carried an evidence bag. "I wonder what evidence they found. Hopefully there's something that will point to the killer."

"Maybe," Eddy said hesitantly. "Since Joel was hit from behind, it's possible that the killer never even touched him, but they will probably be able to get some evidence from the murder weapon."

"Let's hope that Joel didn't see it coming, and that he passed quickly." Samantha shuddered at the thought of the murder.

"We can hope," Eddy replied, though his voice contained a little less sympathy.

"We need to think this through." Walt frowned. "All of this guessing isn't going to get us anywhere."

"Let's go sit for a minute." Samantha gestured to the picnic table not far off. "We can still see anything that Tommy or the investigators are up to."

Samantha led Walt and Eddy over to the picnic table. When she reached it, she sat down and turned to face the villa. What she saw made her freeze for a moment.

"Samantha, did you hear what I said?" Walt asked. "Samantha?"

Samantha stared right into the side window of Joel's villa. "There is a perfect view of the window from here."

"What window?" Eddy leaned his head close to hers in an attempt to see what she was seeing.

"Can you see what I see?" Samantha asked.

"I can see straight into Joel's villa. I am looking straight at the mantle where there is a candlestick. I bet it's the other part of the pair that was used as the murder weapon." Samantha cringed at the thought.

Eddy tilted his head a little more. "I see it now. So, the killer might have sat here and been able to plan what he would use as a murder weapon."

"If he was sitting right in that exact spot." Walt followed the same path with his gaze. "All I see are bushes."

"Maybe he left something behind while he was watching?" Samantha asked with excitement. She stood up from the bench and peered underneath and beside the bench. All she saw was trampled grass and a few strange tracks in the dirt next to the bench.

"Anything?" Eddy asked.

"I don't think so." Samantha shook her head. "I don't know what I was expecting to find anyway. It's pretty clear that whoever sat here could see what was happening inside of Joel's house, but that doesn't mean that the person who killed him sat here."

"I don't know, it would be a pretty good lookout spot." Eddy peered in both directions along the side walk. "There's not much traffic around here, car or foot."

"Good point." Walt looked up suddenly. "Look who's coming." He smiled.

Jo slowly made her way up the hill towards the group. She looked immaculate as always with her long, black hair flowing over her shoulders. Her slender body seemed to effortlessly glide towards them. She eyed the three of them with suspicion.

"Hi Jo!" Samantha waved to her. Jo paused before them and was silent for a moment.

"Oh boy." Jo looked between the three of them.

"What?" Samantha asked.

"The three of you together means you're up to

something." Jo shook her head. "I'm just going to head to my villa."

Eddy chuckled.

"Wait." Samantha stood up. "Why don't you join us? We could use another mind on this situation."

"Another mind? Why, what are you getting yourselves involved in now?" She looked from Eddy to Walt warily. "Actually, never mind, don't tell me. I'll just be on my way." She turned to walk away.

"No problem, we're just trying to solve a murder." Eddy shrugged. "But if you're really not interested, you're not interested."

Jo's eyes widened slightly. Samantha recognized the subtle curve of her lips. She knew that Jo was just as intrigued as the rest of them.

"Well, why didn't you say so?" Jo sat down at the table beside Samantha. "Who is the murderer?"

"I think if we knew that the crime would

already be solved." Eddy made his point with a grim smile.

"All we really know right now is that Joel Westons is dead, and someone killed him last night. He does have a rather troublesome neighbor, Tommy Radner."

"Tommy?" Jo raised an eyebrow. "Is he involved in this?"

"You know him?" Walt asked with surprise. Jo tended to keep to herself. She had slowly become friends with Samantha and mainly tolerated Eddy and Walt. She was not the neighborly type.

"I've had a beer or two with him." Jo nodded.

"Really? With Tommy?" Samantha stared at Jo as if she was trying to figure something out.

"Is that so surprising? He always has something interesting to talk about, and he doesn't care if I just decide to leave." Jo shrugged. "I can't see him as a murderer."

"Well, he has a history with Joel. I've seen the two of them argue before." Samantha frowned.

"Hey, you know more than I do. Tommy and I have never discussed anything personal." Jo looked towards Joel's villa. "I heard about Joel dying, but I didn't realize that it was a murder. Any ideas as to why he was a target?"

"Not just yet." Walt shook his head. "But he was a very successful businessman so I'm hoping something will turn up once I look at his financial history."

"I'm going to find out exactly what kind of trouble Tommy has caused around here. The office staff should know if he'd been harassing the Westons." Samantha stood up from the bench. "I'll catch them before anyone has the chance to slip out for the day."

"Samantha, there should also be some information about whether Tommy ever had complaints from other residents." Eddy stood up as well. "I think the sooner we get to the bottom of all of this, the better."

"Let me know if there's something I can do to

help." Jo turned back towards her villa.

"Now, you're willing to be involved?" Walt asked. "Is that because you know Tommy?"

Jo shot a glance over her shoulder at Walt. She studied him for a moment before answering. "It's because I'm already involved, and I know you'll end up asking anyway. Walt, whatever you might be suspecting, you're way off base." She shook her head a little as she walked away.

"Quite the charmer you are, Walt." Eddy winked at him.

"I was only asking." Walt's eyes widened with innocence.

Samantha left the two men to discuss the difference between honesty and being insulting. She walked down the hill towards the main office. She knew that the woman working would be ready to leave as soon as possible. Ruby was not the talkative type. She did her job and barely got to know the residents. She was quite different from the last person who had held her position.

Samantha didn't mind her standoffish nature normally, but she hoped she would be able to get her talking.

Samantha stepped into the office to find Ruby loading up her purse to leave.

"Ruby, do you have a minute?" Samantha asked. She always made it a point to at least introduce herself to the staff so that if she ever had a problem she would know who to go to.

"I really don't." Ruby picked up her purse. "I was just leaving."

"It will only take a minute." Samantha smiled warmly. "I didn't think you would mind."

"I don't mind, but I do want to get out of here." Ruby slung her purse over her shoulder.

"Because of what happened?" Samantha lowered her voice.

"Yes. I already spoke with the police so I'm going to head home and forget this day ever happened." Ruby frowned. "What is it that you need?"

"What can you tell me about Tommy Radner?" Samantha stood casually beside the desk. She knew that Ruby was not always open or forthcoming with information, but she hoped that in this case she would be.

"That depends, what do you want to know about Tommy?" She looked up at Samantha with concern. "Did he do something to you?" The way she asked the question made Samantha fairly certain that this was not the first time someone had come in to complain.

"He threatened me." Samantha knew that wasn't exactly true, but she figured that it was close enough. "I just want to know if I should take this seriously or not. Do you think he might have just been blowing off some steam?"

"Well, I can't say for sure. All I know is he's had plenty of complaints against him," she explained. "I think he must have some rage issues."

"What about his neighbors, did any of them

ever complain?" Samantha spoke as casually as she could.

"I don't think it's appropriate for me to discuss this, Samantha." Ruby shook her head. "The police have already been given all of that information."

"So, they do suspect Tommy?" Samantha pressed.

"Are you trying to get me fired?" Ruby narrowed her eyes. "Samantha, you're a resident, not a police officer, not a detective, not even a reporter. I can't answer that question for you."

Samantha felt a bit of a hit to the gut at Ruby's words. She had never stopped thinking of herself as a journalist. It wasn't something that she believed anyone could ever actually retire from.

"Thanks for your time." Samantha turned to walk out of the office, but as she neared the door someone was walking in. Samantha's heart lurched as she saw Tommy step into the office. He looked as annoyed as he had earlier in the day.

"I want a new villa," he said flatly without even greeting Ruby or Samantha.

"Excuse me?" Ruby looked up at him with some reluctance.

"I shouldn't have to live next to a crime scene. I shouldn't have to deal with the police and sirens and all of that. I pay good money to live here. I want a new villa." He didn't even look at Samantha. Instead he glared hard at Ruby. "I don't care who you have to talk to, but I want it done, by tonight."

"Tommy, that's impossible. We have very few units open." Ruby tried to remain calm.

"I don't need a few, I just need one. So, get on your phone and make the call to whoever is in charge of you, because I am withholding rent until I get a new, decent place to live. It's bad enough that such crimes are taking place when you advertise a safe place to live. Is it safe when my neighbor gets murdered?" He glowered at her. "Not only that, the other residents are harassing me." He looked directly at Samantha. "This is outrageous. I won't stand for it."

Samantha took a slight step back. There was something about Tommy's anger that seemed more like desperation than frustration. Could it be that he was scared?

"Look Tommy, I'll see what I can do. I can't make any promises." Ruby picked up the phone. Samantha took her cell phone and held it pretending to look at something on it. She made sure it was on silent and she discreetly took a photo of Tommy just as he turned around. She had a feeling she might need it for her investigations. He was becoming more of a suspect by the minute.

"I'm going to be sitting right here." Tommy sat down in one of the leather chairs in the waiting area. "I'll be right here until you get me a new place to live."

He stared hard at Samantha as she made her way past him and out of the office. She was eager to get away from his malicious eyes. A shiver sped up along her spine as the door closed behind her. She had never experienced such an intense feeling of discomfort around someone before. She hurried towards her villa and hoped that Tommy wouldn't follow.

Chapter Four

Eddy took the long walk back towards his villa after parting ways with the others. His mind was churning over the case, but his thoughts were slightly distracted by Jo. He was a little bothered at the idea of her spending time with Tommy. He was not exactly the type of person that Eddy would recommend to anyone as a friend. If he had murdered Joel, Jo could even be in danger. He was bouncing back and forth between the murder and Jo's friendship with Tommy when a voice drew him out of his thoughts.

"Eddy, wait a minute." Abe wheeled up behind him. "Can I talk to you for a minute?"

Eddy turned back to face Abe. "I was just on my way home."

"I understand. I just wanted to see if you found out anything of interest about the murder." Abe looked up at Eddy with a stern stare. Eddy was a little startled by the intensity of his look.

"I didn't find out much I'm afraid. But I'll continue to look into it." He nodded and started to turn to walk away again.

"They don't have a suspect in mind?" Abe asked, his eyes still just as hard.

"Not that I was told." Eddy turned back fully to face him. "You're taking this pretty personally, Abe. Is there something I should know about you and Joel?"

"Like I said we were friends. I just hate to see someone murdered that way." Abe pursed his lips and looked away from Eddy. "It just makes me so angry to think that it could happen here. I mean, when you're in a chair like me, you feel more vulnerable than other people. If someone were to break into my house and try to kill me, how would I get away?" He shook his head.

"I'm sorry, Abe, I hadn't really thought about that." Eddy frowned. "If you're feeling anxious about it maybe you could have someone stay at your place to keep you company."

"I don't need a bunkmate, Eddy," Abe snapped. "What I need is the killer behind bars so that I can feel safe in my home again."

"I can understand that." Eddy shoved his hands into his pockets. "You should know that the murder seemed very personal. So, I don't think there is some kind of serial killer loose in Sage Gardens."

"That's the point isn't it? You don't think." Abe narrowed his eyes. "That's not exactly going to change the fact that I'm not going to be able to sleep tonight."

"Maybe you should talk to someone, Abe." Eddy met his eyes intently. "If it's bothering you this much, maybe you need to discuss these issues with a professional." Eddy felt a rush of sympathy for the man as he suspected that whatever circumstances had led to a life bound to a wheelchair had been traumatic.

"Eddy, just quit your psycho-babble and tell me the truth. Do they have any idea who did this to Joel? I need to know." He looked at Eddy with complete determination. Eddy stared back at him as he slowly processed what he was seeing in Abe's eyes. It was not concern for a friend. Eddy felt a strange sensation of suspicion wash over him.

"What do you have invested in this, Abe?" He felt his interrogator instincts kick in. He could tell that Abe was hiding something.

"Friendship? A sense of security?" Abe huffed and shook his head. "Eddy, I don't even know why I bothered to ask you to help. It's not like you're police anymore. I should just go to the real police to get my answers."

Eddy held back angry words. He could tell that Abe was trying to get him riled up, and he was not going to allow that. He knew how to keep his cool when a situation called for it.

"I don't think that you're being honest with me, Abe. What's really going on here?" Eddy crossed his arms and straightened his shoulders. "Maybe if you told me the truth, I'd be able to help you. Were you and Joel into something together?"

"I have no idea what you're talking about." Abe rolled back a few feet and glared at Eddy. "Forgive me for even thinking that I could ask a friend for help. I won't do it again, Eddy."

Eddy only stared as Abe turned his wheelchair and began heading in the other direction. One of the reasons that Eddy had begun asking questions about the murder was because Abe had asked him to. Now, he wasn't sure what to think about Abe's attitude. He certainly wasn't acting like a grieving friend. Instead he was acting more like a man who had a lot to lose.

**

Samantha stood in her front yard with a small sack filled with birdseed. She needed to calm her nerves after her encounter with Tommy. Feeding the birds was a way she could zone out and let her mind relax. She didn't have that opportunity for long before Eddy walked towards her.

"Hi Samantha." He paused beside her. Samantha didn't look at him, but she did smile in a friendly way. She would have preferred to be alone, but that ship had sailed.

"Hello Eddy, something bothering you?" She offered him the bag of seed.

"Sort of." He shook his head at the bag of seed.

"Do you want to tell me about it?" She knew Eddy was not one to easily volunteer information, but she felt he had come to see her as a bit of a confidant.

Eddy was silent for a moment. When he spoke, his voice was weighted with reluctance. "Abe seems terribly interested in this case."

"You said that he and Joel were friends didn't you?" Samantha asked. She tossed some of the seeds down onto the grass. Various birds

60

swooped down swiftly to snatch them up.

"They were friends I suppose. I don't know but something about it just makes me uneasy." He watched the birds who were making quite a commotion with their flapping wings as they fought over the seed. Always the peacemaker, Samantha tossed more seed to them.

"What are you thinking?" Samantha laughed a little. "That he could have killed Joel? How exactly did he physically manage to climb through the window and hit Joel from behind?"

"Maybe he hired someone," Eddy reached into the bag of seed and grabbed a handful to toss out onto the grass.

"That's possible," Samantha acknowledged.

"It is possible, but unlikely," Eddy said thoughtfully. "It looked like a crime of passion not a professional hit. Unless the murderer made it look like that deliberately."

"But why would Abe want Joel dead? Maybe there's some bad blood between them?"

Samantha held the bag steady as Eddy's rough, thick fingers dug through the seed.

"Maybe," Eddy said thoughtfully. "I also think it's possible that Joel and Abe were involved in something together and Abe is worried that he might be the next victim."

"Like what?" Samantha asked.

"I don't know, but I think we should look into Abe's history, just to quieten my concerns." Eddy spread the seed out across the grass before him. He snapped at one of the larger birds, "Quit being a bully."

Samantha smiled secretively at his soft nature. It wasn't something he revealed too often, but when he did, she felt she was getting a glimpse of the real Eddy beyond the mask he wore.

"I trust your instincts, Eddy. If you think there is something there we should look into it," Samantha agreed. "I had a run in with Tommy. I really think he has a stake in all of this. I wouldn't put it past him to have killed Joel in a fit of rage," she said with disgust. "I didn't get much information from Ruby in the office, but she hinted that some of the residents have had problems with Tommy. If he has an anger problem he might have flown into a rage."

"Maybe." Eddy sighed. He watched the birds fly away. "Do you ever get a feeling about people, Samantha? As if you know something for certain, with no proof of it?"

"Of course. But I've learned I can't rely on that. A hunch is only a hunch until I have some evidence to back it up." She smiled at him. "I learned that from you."

Eddy smiled a little in return. "I guess we've both taught each other a few things."

"I guess you're right. I'm going to check into Abe's background. Something just doesn't feel right about him."

"Let me know if there is anything I can do. I have a few errands to run but I'll have my cell on me." She closed the bag of birdseed and tucked it under her arm.

"Thanks for the talk." Eddy turned and walked off along the water.

Samantha headed back into her villa. As she was stepping through her side door she felt the hairs on the back of her neck stand up. She almost felt as if she was being watched. She scanned the water, but didn't see anyone looking in her direction. With a frown she pulled the door closed firmly behind her.

Chapter Five

Walt settled down in front of his computer. Soft jazz surrounded him as he began to search through Joel's history. He was certain that he would find an explanation for his murder hidden somewhere in his financial history. He had yet to come across a person whose secrets couldn't be revealed by following the money trail they left behind.

As he delved into Joel's history he was surprised at how much information was available to him. Joel was quite a prolific businessman with many of his business ventures documented. He found nothing too out of the ordinary at first. Joel had graduated high in his class in high school and gone on to do well in college. He majored in business and did an apprenticeship with a large corporation right out of college. He was certainly on the path to success. However, Joel seemed to also have luxurious tastes. Not long after he started working and obviously making a reasonable income he was pictured in an article with a particularly expensive watch on his wrist stepping out of a particularly expensive car.

He purchased a home before he was twenty-five and married not long after. The first marriage had failed, but his business success continued. Despite settling a divorce Joel's credit was flawless. By the time he ended up in Sage Gardens he had bought and sold many homes for profit. He had also started several businesses. It was this aspect of Joel's history that Walt began to focus in on. There were many complaints against Joel from business partners and investors.

"That's suspicious," he muttered as he began to notice a pattern of Joel quietly closing or selling off businesses just before their value plummeted. He seemed to know exactly when to get out of a situation. Not only that, he had a flock of investors for each business. He rarely had to risk any of his own capital. His investors were the ones who lost their money.

"Joel, Joel, Joel." Walt shook his head slowly back and forth. "You were a naughty boy."

Walt frowned as he went over the public financial reports of Joel's most recent business once more. He had become so cocky in his ability to make money without investing money that he had begun working in larger amounts. The business he had recently shut down had several investors, each of whom had lost tens of thousands of dollars. That wasn't a small chunk of change to have ripped from your pocket. Joel was so charismatic that it appeared to Walt that his videos and seminars seemed to draw everyone in who saw them. Walt cringed as he realized that a couple of the investors were even residents of Sage Gardens. There was nothing to explain what Joel had done with the money, other than his attempt at fudging the numbers. Walt could see right through that. Joel hadn't deposited most of the investments into the business accounts. The money hadn't been lost to the cost of business as he claimed. Walt presumed that more than likely he had kept it for himself.

"He was running a scheme," Walt said to himself. "That means there is going to be a very long list of people who might be out for revenge." Walt began to look at the complaints of the people who had invested in Joel's business. There were quite a few heartbreaking stories. Some people had lost their savings, while others had lost their homes and businesses. There wasn't a success story out of any of them, aside from Joel himself.

Joel was clever enough to duck the authorities, but that luck would have run out eventually. Instead, Joel had paid the ultimate price. The question was, did he die because of the people he cheated or was the motive something else entirely? All Walt had to work with at the moment was a list of clients who had been wronged, as well as Joel's own incriminating financial history. He thought that would be enough to take to Eddy and Samantha. They might be able to figure out more with their own contacts.

***

After running her errands Samantha returned to her villa. Her mind had been on Anna while she was out. She purchased her a sympathy card and some flowers, but then she felt strange about giving them to her. Knowing how Joel died, could a card and flowers really do anything to ease the pain that Anna was experiencing? She didn't think so. It seemed more like an empty gesture to her.

As Samantha unlocked the door to her villa she felt the same uneasy sensation that she had earlier in the day. She set her purse down on the counter. She looked towards her kitchen window. She was certain that she hadn't left it open, and yet it was open. She shivered a little as the cool evening air wafted into the room.

It occurred to her that someone might be in the villa with her. It was possible that she had opened the window earlier and just forgotten about it. She had done silly things like that before.

She knew that she was probably just being paranoid after learning about the murder, but she wasn't willing to risk it. She flipped the kitchen light on. She took a deep breath and did her best to be intimidating.

"If there is someone in here, you better get out now!" Samantha growled. From the kitchen drawer she pulled out her largest knife. She wasn't about to be taken by surprise. Then she began to make her way through her villa. She checked the bathroom, and the closet. Then she walked into the bedroom. She looked in the closet. Then she jerked up the bed skirt and looked under the bed. When she was sure there was no one in the villa, she sighed with relief.

"You're just being silly, Samantha." She shook her head at her own paranoia. She returned to the kitchen to put the knife away and close the window. She slid the knife back into the drawer. Then she reached up to close the window. When she did she caught sight of a pair of eyes staring back at her. She yelped at the sight and jumped backwards across the kitchen floor.

"Samantha! I'm sorry, are you okay?" Jo asked from outside the window.

"Jo!" Samantha gasped out her friend's name. "What are you doing lurking outside the window?"

"I knocked on the door just before and you weren't home, but I had noticed that your window was open so I was going to close it. It's not safe to have it open when you're not home."

Samantha tried to catch her breath. Her heart was still pounding with fear.

"I know it isn't. Come on in." She reached out and pushed the window closed. Then she opened the side door for Jo. Jo stepped inside with a concerned frown.

"I'm sorry for scaring you."

"It's not your fault. I scared myself." Samantha pulled out one of the chairs at the table and sat down. Jo followed suit. "I swear I didn't leave that window open. I never leave my windows open when I leave the house."

71

"Well, maybe with all of the sirens and excitement you were just distracted?" Jo suggested.

"Maybe," Samantha said dubiously. "It just creeped me out, since Joel's window was left open."

"Did you check the house?" Jo asked.

"Yes. That's what I was doing when you showed up. I just can't believe I freaked myself out so much. I guess the case got to me." Samantha sighed. "Do you want anything to drink?"

"I'll take some water, thank you. Actually, that was why I came by. I wanted to see if you had any update on the situation."

"Not really. Walt was looking into Joel's business and financial history, but I haven't heard from him yet. I can tell you though that Eddy is pretty upset by all of this." Samantha poured Jo a glass of water and handed it to her.

"Eddy? Upset?" Jo looked surprised. "That doesn't seem like him."

"It's not so much that he's upset, I think it's more that he doesn't know what to make of it. It seems to bother him when he can't figure things out." Samantha laughed.

"I could agree with that." Jo sipped her water. As Samantha finished putting her groceries away her phone began to ring.

"Could you see who that is, Jo?" Samantha called out from inside the freezer door.

"Sure." Jo picked up Samantha's phone and checked the caller ID. "It's Eddy."

"Answer it, please!" Samantha gasped as she dropped a box of frozen peas on her foot. Jo frowned. She didn't really want to answer the phone, but she didn't want to ignore Samantha's request either.

"Hello?" she said.

"Who is this?" Eddy asked. "This isn't Samantha."

"No, it isn't." Jo smiled. "It's Jo. Samantha is putting her groceries away."

"Oh," Eddy sounded as if he had no idea how to respond to the unexpected conversation with Jo.

"Did you want me to take a message?" Jo offered.

"Actually, I'd like Samantha and you, if you want, to meet me at Walt's. He's got some information he wants to share about the murder."

"All right, we'll be there in a few." Jo hung up the phone.

"What did he want?" Samantha asked.

"He wants us all to meet at Walt's," Jo replied. She finished her water and then set her glass in the sink.

"Oh good, Walt must have found something." Samantha stowed the last of her groceries. "Shall we head over?"

"Sure." Jo nodded. "Just make sure all your windows are closed."

As Samantha did one more walk through the villa she noticed something odd. On her dresser she kept an assortment of coins and stones she collected from around the lake, as well as other little things. Usually they were in a fairly messy pile. But now they were all swept to one side, as if someone had moved them. Her heart skipped a beat. Was this another sign that someone had been in her villa, or was she just getting forgetful?

"Samantha, you all right?" Jo called from the living room.

"I'll be right there," Samantha called back. She thought about showing Jo what she had found, but she didn't feel confident enough in her own recollection to point a finger at someone breaking in. She shook her head and checked the lock on her bedroom window. It was locked up tight. She turned and walked out of the bedroom, but her stomach was in knots.

"Everything okay?" Jo asked.

Samantha walked past her to the door. "Yes, just overthinking everything." She frowned.

"Soon enough we'll get to the bottom of this

and then you won't have to overthink anything anymore."

"I hope so." Samantha took one last glance over her shoulder before closing the door.

***

When Samantha and Jo arrived at Walt's house, Eddy was standing at the end of the driveway.

"Samantha, are you feeling okay?" Eddy tilted his head to the side. "You're looking a little pale."

"I'm fine," Samantha mumbled. "Is Walt inside?"

"Yes, I figured I'd wait for you. I just got here a moment ago. Hello, Jo." He nodded to Jo.

"Eddy." She nodded in return. Samantha was pleased by how they could almost civilly greet each other.

"Let's see what Walt found out." Samantha

walked up to the door and knocked firmly.

Walt opened the door almost as soon as Samantha knocked.

"Oh good, you're here." He waved the three of them inside. "I've found out some intriguing information about Joel."

"What is it?" Eddy asked. Walt walked over to his computer desk. He sat down in the rolling chair and gestured for everyone to come closer.

"He might have been a successful businessman, but it wasn't from being an honest one." Walt gestured to the screen on his computer. "There was a lawsuit pending, brought against him by several of his investors. Apparently, Joel was great at generating funding for starting a business, but not so great at actually creating returns for his investors."

"He wasn't as great a businessman as he seemed?" Samantha frowned as she peered at the legal jargon on the screen. "Was he having financial trouble?"

"Actually, no he wasn't. He was living just fine. But he was running some sort of scheme and his investors lost quite a bit of money. Enough to cause some of them to lose their own businesses, homes, everything." He sighed. "It's heartbreaking to see that kind of financial loss. People work so hard to get what they have, and then it is just gone."

Samantha was a little surprised when she noticed a hint of tears in Walt's eyes. She knew that he took his work seriously as an accountant, but she didn't quite comprehend his relationship with finances.

"So, he was a con artist?" Jo asked from behind Walt. "Sounds like he got what was coming to him."

"Jo!" Walt looked at her reproachfully.

"What?" Jo asked sternly. "It's not like I did the deed myself, but he set himself up to be attacked. You can't get away with fleecing people of all their money forever. He had to have known that eventually he was going to face some consequences."

"Maybe he thought about jail time, or even getting beat up. I doubt that he expected to be murdered in his living room." Eddy clenched his teeth for a moment, and then he sighed. "It looks like there is a lot more to this than any of us realized. It's not going to be so simple with such a large suspect pool."

"I'm sure I can narrow it down some," Samantha offered. "Most people will have an alibi for the time of the murder, and those that don't might have other ways to prove that they weren't involved. Let's sit down and get a list together. You can do a criminal check on them, Eddy, and I'll go through their past."

"I've already looked through the financials to figure out who were the hardest hit." Walt selected the print option. "A couple on the list actually live in Sage Gardens. He must have drummed up some investors here. One in particular I believe you may find interesting."

Eddy snatched the paper out of the printer. He skimmed over the list, then saw a name that made him freeze.

"Who is it?" Samantha asked.

"Tommy Radner," Eddy read from the printed sheet of paper.

"Tommy Radner was one of the investors in Joel's bad business?" Samantha asked with wide eyes.

"Yes, but not for much. Really, the amount he invested didn't cause him much financial damage. However, since he is our main suspect, I thought it best to include him." Walt frowned. "I'm not sure a few hundred dollars would be enough reason for him to murder Joel."

"Maybe not, but it could be a culmination of things," Jo pointed out.

"She's right." Samantha nodded. "Tommy himself told us that he didn't like Joel much. Then he had problems with them as neighbors, and on top of it all Joel lost the money he invested. Even though it wasn't much, it might have been the tipping point for Tommy. Maybe he'd had enough, and his anger caused him to act out."

"It's very possible," Eddy agreed. "Someone with that kind of rage can easily fly off the handle and do things that they would regret."

"When I spoke to Ruby in the office today, Tommy was demanding another villa," Samantha recalled with narrowed eyes. "I bet he is trying to distance himself just in case he left any evidence of the crime behind."

"That would be clever of him," Eddy remarked. "If he gets moved to another villa then any evidence found in his villa, if he's investigated, will be considered at risk of being tampered with because he no longer has possession of the villa. Tommy seems to be pretty determined to cover up his tracks."

"I think it's time we find out if he really went to the movies," Samantha said with a slight smile. "What do you think, Walt, would you like to join me?"

"I'd love to." Walt nodded. Eddy looked between the two warily.

"Are you sure that anyone will even remember him?" Jo inquired with some scepticism.

"If he acted anything like himself, then he would have made quite an impression." Samantha was hopeful that Tommy would have had a run-in with someone at the movies.

"Don't you think the police would have already looked into his alibi?" Walt asked. "I mean, they have to have some of the same information that we do. Wouldn't they have followed up already?"

"Maybe, but that doesn't mean that the information they received is valid. I'd like to hear it with my own ears." Samantha crossed her arms. "Walt and I will head over to the theater for the last show, that was the time when Tommy claims to have been seeing a movie."

"He also insisted that I did not see him there,"

Walt recalled. "He was so certain of it. To me that means that either he wasn't there, or he was doing his best to conceal his presence."

"I would guess it was the first option," Samantha suggested.

"I'll just go get ready and I'll meet you back here in about half an hour so we can make the last showing," Samantha suggested.

"Okay," Walt said as he glanced at his watch.

"Are you sure you don't want me to come along?" Eddy offered.

Jo patted him on the shoulder. "Trust me they're better off without you, Eddy. You still look like a cop. People don't like to talk to cops."

"I don't think I really look like a cop," Eddy muttered as Jo led him out the door and Samantha followed.

"I think you could be wearing leather pants and a blue wig and you would still look like a cop." Jo laughed.

Chapter Six

After the three friends left Walt's villa Samantha headed in one direction towards her villa while Eddy and Jo walked in the other direction. As soon as Jo's feet hit the walkway she sped her pace up a bit. She didn't want Eddy to feel obligated to walk beside her. As she expected, Eddy made no attempt to match her pace. She headed in the direction of her villa. She always felt strange when she was alone with Eddy. She was trying to get more comfortable with him, but it was difficult when their backgrounds clashed so much, with Eddy having been a cop and Jo having been a cat burglar. She was about to turn down the path that led to her villa when she felt a hand lightly grasp her elbow. She fought her instinct to turn and punch. Instead she looked over her shoulder.

"I thought you might like to brainstorm at my place," Eddy suggested. "I can use my connections at the department to do some investigating into Tommy's past. I could use a sounding board. What do you say?" He met her eyes with a hint of hope in his.

"Are you sure?" She frowned. "I'm certain that you could handle that by yourself."

"Maybe. But it's always good to have a different perspective on things. You can help look up some stuff on the internet." He gestured down the path towards his villa. "I have burgers."

"Burgers you say?" Jo raised an eyebrow. "Now that might be a good enough reason."

"Great." He smiled. "I can have them ready in one minute and thirty seconds."

Jo resisted the urge to groan. She hadn't realized that he was referring to microwavable hamburgers. Still, she was touched that he had made the offer. She nodded. "All right. Let's see what Tommy has to hide."

They fell easily into step together. Eddy's villa was not far, it was still fairly light outside when they reached it. He opened the door for Jo. Jo stepped inside and picked her way past Eddy's favorite chair. She was tempted to sit in it just to ruffle his feathers, but she decided to play nice. She sat down instead at his cluttered dining room table. She noticed there were all kinds of folders stacked in messy piles.

"What are these?" She began to pick up one of the folders.

"Drop it!" Eddy spoke gruffly. Jo immediately dropped the folder and looked over at him with concern. "What's the problem?"

"They're files. Cold cases." He shrugged. "Sometimes, if I'm feeling a yearning for some police work I'll have one of the guys bring over a few files for me to look through. But I'd prefer that you not touch them."

"Okay." She nodded. Just from a glance she could count at least ten folders. She could safely assume that he had been having quite a few yearnings for the old days lately. She looked up at him with a different level of understanding. Letting go of the past was hard for Eddy, too. He sat down at the table beside her and handed her a beer.

"So, what do you think you can find out about Tommy?" Jo asked.

"I put a call through to my friend, Chris, who works at the station. He's a lab technician, but he's got his hands in everything. I asked him to see if he could dig up anything on Tommy. If he does, he'll let me know. But not all bad behavior is reported to the police. I thought we could check into whether Tommy has had any civil complaints. We can see if we can find out how deep the animosity between Tommy and Joel was."

"That's a good idea." Jo took a sip of her beer. She didn't drink very often, but she felt comfortable to do so with Eddy. "I'll look up what I can on my phone," Jo offered. She pulled out her cell phone and began doing some searches on Tommy. While she skimmed the results, Eddy's phone began to ring.

"It's Chris." Eddy nodded. "Just give me a

minute." He stood up and walked down the hallway to his bedroom. Jo thought it was odd that he required so much privacy for the conversation. To her it was yet another sign that he did not trust her.

"Chris, thanks for doing this," Eddy spoke in a low voice as he closed his bedroom door.

"Anything for you, Eddy, you know that. I did find a few things on Tommy."

"What did you find?" Eddy asked.

"Mostly minor scuffles, but Tommy has a habit of getting into fistfights. He's been arrested for disorderly conduct a few times, but the charges were dismissed. He hasn't caused any serious injuries that are on record, but he did have a domestic dispute listed from ten years ago. However, those charges were dropped as well."

"Hmm, it seems like he's gotten away with losing his temper plenty of times before, seems like he is a loose cannon that could have committed the murder. What do you think?" He paused and listened closely. He valued Chris' opinion on cases more than many detectives. Though he was young and rather inexperienced he had a clear mind and strong instincts. He also knew how to find out whatever information he wanted on just about anyone.

"I don't know, Eddy. Even though he had multiple arrests none of them led to any real injuries. Even the domestic dispute was over possessions rather than a physical attack. He certainly doesn't seem like the calmest guy around, but going from breaking a few lamps to bashing someone's head in, is a big leap," he sounded unconvinced.

"That's a good point." Eddy grimaced. He had hoped that whatever Chris found would lead to a fairly cut and dry answer. "Have you heard anything from the medical examiner?"

"Actually, yes. The exam showed that whoever killed Joel was strong and likely a little taller than Joel. The blows were harsh and did a lot of damage. Also, there was likely a large amount of blood splatter on the attacker."

"That makes the wife a very unlikely suspect," Eddy remarked thoughtfully.

"I'd say so." Chris paused a moment and then spoke quickly. "Listen Eddy, this is about all of the information I can offer you about this case. It's been assigned to a senior detective."

"I understand," Eddy replied quietly. Chris was a little concerned about being caught, and he had good reason to be. Many of the older detectives were aware that Eddy used Chris as a contact. Most didn't care, but if they did anything to foul up the detective's investigation, Chris would be the one to pay the price. "Thanks for what you've done already."

"Whatever I can do, I will do." Chris hung up the phone. Eddy tucked his phone back into his pocket and walked back out to join Jo. He found her studying the books on his bookshelf. Eddy quickly tried to remember whether there was anything on that shelf that he wouldn't want Jo looking at.

"Find anything interesting?" He stepped up beside her.

"Just surprised at some of your choices." Jo shot him a small smile. "I didn't peg you for a reader."

"Really?" Eddy met her eyes. "Do I not look studious to you?"

Jo did her best not to laugh in reaction to the question. "So, what did your contact have to say?"

Eddy blinked as if he had just remembered what they were dealing with.

"Oh right. Our Tommy Radner has a criminal record." He sat down at the table. "He's been in a good amount of trouble in the past."

"Well, that points to him being the killer." Jo sat down across from him. "But if the police have this information why hasn't he been picked up yet?"

"The previous arrests were all for minor crimes. Some did involve minimal violence. The police may not feel that is enough to create a case against him just yet." He sat back in his chair. "To be honest I'm not sure it's enough for me either. I just feel that if a man is going to be violent enough to kill he doesn't get into arguments without really causing harm."

"Yes, but these arrests were in the past. Things could have happened since then to trigger his rage. Maybe bad circumstances piled up to the point that he just snapped," Jo suggested. "It's hard to imagine, but it happens."

"That may be it." Eddy nodded slowly. He still felt as if something wasn't quite right. He couldn't place what made him uneasy about Tommy as a suspect. "Still, is he a killer?"

"Can anyone really tell if someone else is a killer?" Jo questioned. "It's not as if they wear a sign."

"Maybe not, but I have seen the coldness in the eyes of a murderer. It's something I've never seen in the eyes of another human being." He closed his eyes for a moment as he recalled the cruel men that he had placed in handcuffs. "But I don't see that coldness in Tommy's eyes. All I see is bitterness."

"Hm. Maybe you're getting rusty," Jo asked, hoping Eddy would take the bait.

"Don't even think it," Eddy replied mockingly. "I thought you didn't suspect Tommy?"

"I don't suspect anyone, as a rule. The guilty party will show him or herself given time." She smiled with confidence.

"Interesting." Eddy knocked his knuckles against the table. "I think I might like that philosophy."

Chapter Seven

After getting changed to go to the theater Samantha knocked on Walt's door. Walt opened the door almost immediately.

"Come in," Walt gestured. Samantha walked into his villa. Walt shifted uncomfortably as if he was a bit nervous being alone with her. "Well, would you like me to drive?" he offered.

"If you don't mind. I prefer not to drive at night, unless I have to," Samantha explained.

"I don't mind. I prefer to be driving if I'm in a car." Walt smiled. Samantha was not surprised. She wondered how their evening would go, considering that Walt needed everything to be just right.

"I'll just get my wallet." Walt walked into the back bedroom.

Alone in Walt's living room Samantha took a good look around. She noticed that there were three photographs on an otherwise empty wall.

Each photograph was perfectly aligned to be in a straight row. Inside each of the frames the image was of a single flower. The first flower was just a bud. The second was in bloom. The third was wilting. Samantha found something fascinating about the photographs. She was still staring at them when Walt walked back in.

"Ready?" he asked.

"Sure." Samantha nodded. "Did you take these?"

"Yes, I did." Walt stared at the pictures for a moment. "It was for a school project when I was in high school. I liked how the pictures turned out, so they have travelled with me ever since."

Samantha smiled. She knew that Walt's particular ways had a purpose. She was glad to see that he also had a more creative side.

"We better go!" Walt declared.

Once Samantha was settled in Walt's little car she felt as if she was sitting in a cloud. Not only did he have the air conditioning set at exactly the right temperature, his car looked like it had a daily vacuum. There was not a crumb or a crumpled up receipt to be found.

"Nice car, Walt." She smiled at him.

"It's top rated for safety," Walt explained. "I'm not taking any chances. If I happen to get into an accident, which is statistically possible, then I want my injuries to be as minimal as possible."

Samantha offered him an admiring nod before looking back out the window. The streetlights were just beginning to come on. The sun was slipping behind the trees. She felt a strange sense of sadness. Joel would not witness another sunset, or sunrise. Sometimes she focused a little too much on the crime, and not the victim. Joel was a person. He might not have been the best person in the world, but he was still a person. He was a husband, too.

"What are you thinking about?" Walt asked. He kept his eyes fixated on the road before him.

"Oh, I was just thinking about Joel," she

admitted quietly.

"What about him?" Walt asked. His gaze remained ever vigilant through the windshield.

"Just that he won't see another sunrise. He'll never have the opportunity to make the right choice."

"The right choice? I don't think Joel ever would have done that. He seemed to enjoy the money he was earning from making the wrong choices."

"Maybe so, but people do change, sometimes. Maybe if he had lived for another ten years he could have done a complete turnaround." She sighed and then looked over at Walt. "I guess a part of me always thinks about the story that has yet to be written."

Walt turned into the parking lot of the movie theater. "That's noble, Samantha, but you have to remember, that unwritten story could have ended in a multitude of ways, including Joel's criminal behavior escalating to the point of causing even more destruction. In your ideal version Joel would grow a conscience, but that is only one potential outcome, and not a very likely one." He parked the car and turned to look at her. "Your optimism is refreshing, Samantha, but statistically…"

"All right, all right." Samantha stepped out of the car and onto the path that led up to the front of the theater. Walt fell into step beside her. As they walked up to the ticket booth, Samantha noticed that the woman behind the glass was only half-awake. That did not bode well for her remembering whether Tommy was there last night.

"Excuse me, miss?" Walt did not get too close to the glass. When the woman didn't respond he wrapped a tissue around his hand and knocked lightly. The woman jerked awake. She stared between Walt and Samantha with some confusion, and then as if she remembered where she was, she sat up.

"What show?" she asked.

"Actually, we're not here to buy a ticket. We'd like some information." Walt smiled.

The woman stared at him with disbelief. "I sell tickets, if you're not here to buy one, then you'll have to move along."

"What if we offer to buy information?" Samantha slid a twenty dollar bill through the small opening at the base of the glass. Walt looked at her reproachfully, but she ignored him. During her time as a journalist she had learned that greasing palms was a great way to get a person talking.

"Oh, uh, what kind of information?" The woman picked up the twenty and looked at it hesitantly.

"All I want to know is if you saw this man here last night." Samantha held her phone up to the glass. It had the photograph of Tommy that she had snapped earlier at the office.

The woman peered through the glass.

"He looks familiar." She frowned. "I see a lot

of people come and go though."

"This would have been at the last show last night." Samantha continued to hold up her phone. "Just do your best to remember." She didn't want to sway the woman's memory one way or the other, she wanted an honest answer.

"I just can't quite." The woman sighed. "You know, wait just a minute. I think I do remember him. Actually, I think I remember who he was with." She snapped her fingers. "I bet I'm right. But Jerry would know better than me. He works at the snack counter inside. Go ahead in and you can ask him." She pointed to the door. Samantha smiled with gratitude, but she was disappointed. Tommy's alibi was that he was at the movies alone, she could not have been remembering the right person if she thought he was with someone. Walt held open the door for Samantha.

"This is a waste of time," he warned. Samantha knew that he had come to the same conclusion that she had.

"Let's just follow it through and see where it leads. I already spent the twenty." She winked lightly at him.

"Which was a mistake," Walt spoke with a hint of displeasure in his voice. Samantha ignored it. She couldn't expect a retired accountant to understand bribery. She had learned it had its place, especially when she had very few other ways to convince someone to tell her the truth. At the snack counter a young man was fighting with the popcorn machine. Hot air was blowing, but the popcorn was not popping.

"It must be clogged again," he muttered.

"Excuse me, Jerry?" Samantha asked.

The young man turned to look at Samantha and Walt. "Sorry guys, if you're looking for popcorn it's going to be a few minutes."

"No, thank you." Walt tilted his head towards Samantha's phone. "We'd like you to take a look at this picture."

"The woman at the ticket window said you

might remember this man from last night, or someone he was with." Samantha held up her phone.

Jerry stared at it for a moment. Then he broke out into a smile.

"Oh yes, I remember them." He nodded.

"Are you sure?" Samantha asked with some confusion. "He was with someone else?"

"Yes, in fact I never would have noticed him if it wasn't for her. She was quite the firecracker." He laughed.

"What does that mean?" Walt asked.

"Well, the guy wanted to just go straight to the theater. He was kind of pulling her along with him. She started insisting that she wanted popcorn. He started getting aggravated. She barked at him that if he was going to take her on a date he had to treat her right and buy her snacks." Jerry laughed again. "That's when I started paying attention, because I just thought it was funny that she would demand snacks."

"A date?" Samantha repeated. She exchanged a look of confusion with Walt before looking back at Jerry. "So, did he buy her snacks?"

"Sure he did. The woman was quite a looker, you know, an older lady, but still gorgeous, like you." He smiled charmingly at Samantha.

Walt raised an eyebrow.

Samantha tried to ignore the flattery. "So, she was about my age?"

"Yes, I'd say so." Jerry nodded. "She made him buy her popcorn and a drink. I thought it was a little odd that he didn't buy himself anything. I figured he was just being cheap."

"Did they argue?" Walt asked.

"Not really, he just kind of gave in to what she wanted, and then hurried her away to the theater. I don't know why he was in such a rush, they were early for the show by about twenty minutes." He shrugged. "Maybe he didn't want to miss the previews."

"Did he ever say the woman's name?" Samantha asked.

"No. That was the other odd thing, he just kept calling her doll. I mean they were an older couple, but who calls their girlfriend doll anymore? I can tell you if I called my girlfriend doll she would punch me right in the nose." He laughed loudly.

"You don't have a girlfriend do you, Jerry?" Walt asked.

"Uh well, not currently. Anyway, I really have to fix this popcorn machine." He cast a wink in Samantha's direction. "If you wait until it's fixed, I'll give you a free bag."

Walt wrapped an arm around Samantha's shoulders and steered her away from the counter. "Thanks, we have to be on our way."

As they walked out of the movie theater Samantha shrugged Walt's arm off. "What was that about?" she asked with an amused grin.

"That boy was clearly flirting with you, I was just saving you the trouble of having to turn him down." Walt unlocked the car.

"And what if I didn't want to turn him down?" Samantha asked incredulously.

"Oh?" Walt paused and met her eyes with an unreadable expression. "I didn't take you for the type that favored pimples and helping with homework."

"Walt! He was at least twenty." Samantha laughed out loud.

"Statistically, May December relationships do not last." Walt opened Samantha's door for her.

"More like January December." Samantha giggled. She couldn't deny that the young man's attention had been a little flattering. She sat down in the car and began flipping through her phone.

"What are you looking for?" Walt asked. Samantha was still skimming through her phone.

"When I was trying to get into the group that runs the social activities at Sage Gardens I got a lot of the contact information for the women who are members. I've never deleted them because contacts are contacts."

"That still doesn't tell me what you're looking for," Walt pointed out.

"Oh well, something Jerry said made me think of someone." She paused for a moment and stared down at her phone.

"What is it?" Walt asked. He squeezed the steering wheel anxiously. He wanted to look over at Samantha, but refused to take his eyes off the road.

"Yes, there is a woman who lives at Sage Gardens. Her name is Cynthia Doll. But all of the ladies just called her Doll." Samantha looked over at Walt. "When Jerry said that Tommy was calling his date doll that seemed odd to me. I can't see Tommy ever calling someone doll, unless that was her name." She smiled a little. "I also couldn't imagine Doll dating Tommy, but maybe she likes her men with a little bit of attitude. I know plenty of women that do."

Walt suddenly stepped on the brake.

Samantha was jolted forward but her seatbelt kept her from moving too much.

"Sorry!" Walt gulped. "I got distracted."

"It's okay." Samantha adjusted her seatbelt. "I think we need to have a conversation with Tommy and with Doll."

"The question is, if Tommy was at the movies with this Cynthia Doll last night, then why didn't he tell the police that? Why did he claim he was alone? Jerry said he was trying to hurry Doll along. It was like he was trying to keep from being seen," Walt said perplexed.

"I can tell you why," Samantha replied smugly. "Because there is a Mr. Doll."

"Oh." Walt's eyes widened. "They are having an affair."

"So, it seems," Samantha agreed, "unless I am off base in thinking that the Doll he was with last night was Cynthia Doll. Tommy's going to have to admit to it, because there's no way that Doll will do anything to tarnish her perfect image."

"Sounds like a job for Eddy." Walt drove into Sage Gardens. It was nearing eleven o'clock, much later than he was used to being out. "I can call him in the morning," he offered.

"That's all right, I'll let him know." Samantha smiled as Walt parked in her driveway. "Have a good night, Walt."

"Thanks." Walt watched as she walked up the path to her front door. He waited until she had unlocked her door and was safely inside. Then he began the drive to his villa. As he did, he noticed something odd. Abe was rolling along the sidewalk. Walt slowed down a little and considered asking him if he was okay. But then he stopped himself. Abe had every right to be out as late as he wanted to, a wheelchair didn't stop him from being able to go out. Still it seemed odd to Walt that he would be out wandering so late. Abe didn't seem to be concerned. He looked quite relaxed as he rolled down the path. Walt assumed he must be going to visit someone. He gave a slight wave through the window. If Abe noticed, he didn't respond. Walt continued down the road with his mind on Joel.

Chapter Eight

Samantha stepped into her villa and felt immediate apprehension. She had almost forgotten about the strange occurrences from earlier. First she had found a window open that she was certain she had closed, and then she had found the items on the top of her dresser pushed aside. All of this came rushing back to her as she stared into her dark villa. She stood just inside the door and flicked the light on. The room filled with light, revealing that everything was just as she had left it. She still shivered a little.

To help ease her nervousness she decided to give Eddy a call. He was often awake fairly late and she wanted to update him on what had happened at the movie theater. She dialed his number as she poured herself a glass of juice. Eddy answered on the first ring.

"Sam, is everything okay?" Eddy asked with some urgency.

"Yes, I just wanted to let you know what we found out tonight." Samantha suppressed a yawn. "It's not too late I hope."

"Not at all," Eddy replied. "In fact Jo and I are still going over some of the information I found out about Tommy's background."

"Oh, Jo is there with you?" Samantha was surprised. Eddy and Jo hadn't been very quick to be friendly with one another. She was also relieved. The more comfortable Eddy became with Jo the less tension there would be between the four of them.

"Yes. We were trying to come up with any previous evidence of Tommy's volatile temper. So far we've had a few hits."

"I think you might have wasted your time." Samantha sighed. "I'm fairly certain that Tommy's alibi is solid."

"Really?" Eddy asked. "What did you find out? I didn't think much would come from your visit."

"I didn't either, but apparently Tommy and the

woman he was with made quite an impression on the employees." She sipped her juice.

"Tommy had a date?" Eddy sounded surprised. "Who would go out with a man like him?"

"Possibly a socialite by the name of Doll." Samantha smiled into the phone. "She has to be the most prim and proper woman that lives in Sage Gardens, but it looks like she's been stepping out on her husband. I thought you might want to have a talk with Tommy about it in the morning."

"I'll do just that," Eddy agreed. "But it's disappointing that now our only suspect is Anna. I still don't think she would be strong enough to pull off something like this."

"Maybe not. But she could have hired someone to do it. And don't forget the list of suspects that Walt gave us." Samantha sighed as she thought of the list. It was going to take a lot of digging to get to the bottom of it.

"I still think Abe is a little too interested in the case. Maybe he's connected somehow?" Eddy suggested.

"I can look into his past and see what I can find," Samantha offered. "I'm going to turn in for the night though."

"Okay, rest well, Sam."

"Thanks, you too, Eddy. Tell Jo I said goodnight."

"Will do."

After Eddy hung up the phone he turned to look at Jo. She was finishing the cup of tea he had made her not long before. "Looks like we can cross Tommy off our list of suspects. I'm going to have a conversation with him in the morning to confirm it, but it looks like he was at the movies with a married woman."

"Really," Jo said with surprise. "Are you sure he couldn't have got back in time to kill Joel?"

"I don't think so. Besides, it really looks like a crime of passion. It would take an awful lot of planning to pull off creating an alibi and committing a murder all while not slipping up. I don't think he has the smarts for it. Do you?"

"Well, Tommy never did strike me as a murderer." Jo sipped the last of her tea. "But I guess we'll find out for sure. I wouldn't be too harsh with him though, or he might end up being a thorn in your side."

"Tommy doesn't frighten me," Eddy's voice was stern. He stood up and took the empty mug.

"I didn't mean to imply that he did. I just think he could get pretty annoying after a while, and a man like him tends to hold a grudge." Jo stood up from the table.

"Just how much do you know about what kind of man Tommy is?" Eddy turned to look at Jo inquisitively.

"What are you asking me, Eddy?" Jo's eyes danced with a touch of amusement. She paused just in front of Eddy and held his gaze boldly.

"I'm asking what business you had with him

that allowed you such an intimate understanding of him." Eddy didn't back down. Instead he took a small step closer. "You don't seem to like him very much, but you also know quite a lot about him."

"Is this the part where you start to question my motives again?" Jo asked in a disappointed tone. "I don't know what I have to do to prove my friendship, Eddy, but I'm also not interested in finding out. Either you consider me a friend, or you don't consider me at all."

"My friends tend to be fairly forthcoming. I asked you a simple question." Eddy scowled.

"I'm not under your interrogation, Eddy I'm not obligated to answer your questions. As your friend, I can tell you that I associated with Tommy because he had a connection I needed in the gardening community. I wanted a certain kind of flower, and he knew the person to get it from. Does that put your mind at ease?" She stepped around him and towards the door.

"Jo, wait." Eddy turned to face her. "Look, old

habits die hard."

"Once a cat burglar, always a cat burglar, I'm used to the routine." Jo shook her head. "I thought maybe we had gotten past that, Eddy."

"It's not that at all. Well, maybe a little." Eddy shrugged. "I don't trust easily, Jo. It's nothing personal."

"So, don't trust. That doesn't mean we can't be friends, does it?" Jo met his eyes. "Do you really think I trust you?"

Eddy stared back at her as the tension built between them. No matter how he tried, he couldn't quite figure Jo out. One moment she was as casual as the next door neighbor, the next he could see the cunning in her that had allowed her to survive on the run. It was hard to reconcile those two personalities.

"So, we don't trust each other. Friendship usually requires that we do." Eddy frowned.

"Does it? I don't think so." Jo looked towards the door for a moment and then back at Eddy.

"Actually, that's something to think about. We've all been looking at Joel's enemies, but what about his friends?"

Eddy realized that she was trying to change the subject, but he didn't stop her. He had gotten himself into a conversation that there was no real way out of.

"I think you're right. It just brings my thoughts back to Abe." Eddy shook his head. "You probably think I'm a lunatic for even considering a man in a wheelchair as a possibility."

"Not at all." Jo levelled her gaze on Eddy. "I'm always amazed at what people are capable of doing, Eddy. Where there is a will there usually is a way."

She turned and walked out of Eddy's villa. As the door closed behind her she felt her heart drop slightly. Just when she thought she was making progress, beginning to be accepted, Eddy had made it clear that he still viewed her as a threat. It was frustrating, to say the least.

Chapter Nine

Samantha woke up the next morning with a feeling of dread. She immediately looked towards her bedroom window. It was closed and locked just as she had left it. Still, she felt nervous as she climbed out of bed. It was early enough that the villa was still mostly dim. She made her way slowly into the kitchen. The first thing that she noticed were the curtains moving over her kitchen sink. Her stomach tightened with fear. Her eyes flew wide open as she watched the curtains swing in the breeze. The window was open all the way. She was certain that she had not left it open. She hadn't even opened it since Jo had startled her. Samantha quickly looked around the villa. She checked in closets, even in cabinets, and behind furniture. There was no sign of anyone else inside the villa.

Samantha grabbed her purse and searched for her cell phone. She wanted to get someone else on the phone before she lost her mind. The more she searched in her purse the more frustrated she became. There were plenty of receipts, crumpled up wrappers, and loose change, but there was no cell phone. Samantha growled with frustration. Then she spotted her phone sitting on the kitchen counter not far from the open window. Had she left it there? She rarely left her phone out in the open. She didn't remember leaving it there. But then she had come in late from the movies with Walt. She had been tired when she talked to Eddy on the phone. Perhaps she had laid it down and forgotten to pick it back up.

It didn't explain the open window, but it made sense that she might have left the phone there. She reached for the phone. Before she could grasp it, the phone began ringing. She gasped with surprise. The phone was just doing what it was supposed to do, but she had been so uptight that the shrill ring scared her. She saw that it was Eddy calling.

"Hello?" Samantha's voice shook slightly.

"Samantha, is it too early?" Eddy asked. "I had trouble sleeping."

"No, it's not too early." Samantha held tightly onto the phone. She stared at the open window.

"I'm going to talk to Tommy this morning. I just wanted to check in with you before I did. I also want to ask you for a favor," Eddy sounded determined.

"What is it?" Samantha asked.

"I know it seems like a long shot, but I'd like you to look into Abe. Dig as deep as you can. I just can't shake this feeling I have about him."

"No problem, I'll do a thorough search. Why don't we meet up after you speak to Tommy?" Samantha suggested. She was hoping to spend as little time alone as possible.

"Sure." Eddy paused a moment. "Are you okay, Samantha?" His voice deepened with concern.

"I think so." Samantha reached up and closed the window. She made sure that it was securely locked. She didn't want to admit to being afraid. If she did Eddy wouldn't leave her alone about it. She wanted to be sure that what she was experiencing was real before she told anyone else.

"Do you want to come with me to talk to Tommy?" he offered. Samantha could sense that he was really just offering her company.

"No, I'll get to work on Abe. If your instincts are telling you that there is something strange there, I believe you." Samantha sat down in front of her computer. She could get her coffee later. She needed something to take her mind off the fear that she was feeling.

"All right, I'll see you in a little while." Eddy hung up the phone.

He looked at the screen for a moment as if hoping it would give him more of an explanation about the conversation he had just had. Samantha was clearly disturbed by something, but she wasn't willing to tell him about it. He wondered if Jo wasn't the only one that felt judged by him. He pushed the thought out of his mind and headed out the front door. He wanted to catch Tommy before he had the chance to go out for the day. As he walked up to Tommy's villa he could see that he had made it just in time. There was a moving truck at Tommy's. Tommy himself was standing at the end of his driveway with his hands on his hips. He was watching the movers like a hawk.

"Be careful with that television," he snapped.

"Tommy!" Eddy called out to him as he walked closer.

"What do you want?" Tommy sighed.

"I see that you're moving." Eddy nodded towards the truck.

"You really are quite the detective." Tommy sneered in Eddy's direction.

"Moving closer to Doll's place then?" Eddy asked casually.

Tommy turned to look at him so quickly that

Eddy heard a subtle cracking sound from the man's neck.

"What did you just say?" he demanded.

"I could ask you about it, or I could ask her husband where he thinks she was last night." Eddy narrowed his eyes and squared his shoulders. He was sending a clear message to Tommy that he would not be intimidated.

Tommy's face paled. He clenched his jaw and looked back at the movers. When he spoke again it was through tightened lips. "How do you know about that?"

"Does it really matter how I know?" Eddy replied brusquely. "All that matters is whether it's true, and who finds out, right?"

"It's true," Tommy huffed. "But it isn't anyone's business. I don't know how anyone found out!"

"That's why you said you were alone at the movies? You were trying to hide your affair?" Eddy asked. Tommy raised his hand to shush him as the movers carried a mattress out to the truck.

Once they had disappeared back inside he turned back to Eddy.

"Look. It isn't an affair. At least not yet. We're just trying things out. I didn't want anyone to know, she's got a lot to lose. I even cut my own hair so that no one would recognize me," he said softly. "I didn't want to put her in the position to have to explain to her husband what she was doing at the movies with me. That's why I told the police I was alone. But it doesn't change the fact that I didn't kill anyone."

"You say." Eddy tilted his head towards Anna's house. "Maybe you are using Cynthia as your cover, to prove that you weren't here killing Joel?"

"Listen, you're really imaginative, with this little fantasy you have in your mind. I had nothing to do with Joel's death. If I was going to use Cynthia as an alibi then why would I lie about her being there?" He glared at Eddy. "Why don't you go find a job at a department store as the greeter or something so you can keep yourself occupied?

Running around here playing detective isn't cutting it."

"Watch it." Eddy glared right back at him.

"Watch what?" Tommy scowled at him. "What are you going to do, cuff me?" Tommy started to turn back towards the house. Eddy was doing his best to control his temper, he knew that Tommy was just trying to goad him into a fight. He'd gotten the confirmation that he needed. Tommy was at the movies with Cynthia Doll. It was very unlikely that he killed Joel. He was just about to walk away when Tommy suddenly spun around.

"Maybe you should ask Anna who she thinks killed her husband," Tommy snapped. "I'm sure she has a pretty good idea."

"Why do you say that?" Eddy asked with interest.

"A woman like Anna gets swept up in romance. Not that I blame her with the way Joel treated her, but I'm betting whoever she was getting attention from had something to do with this." He pointed at the pile of garbage at the curb of Anna and Joel's old villa. "A loving wife doesn't do that, now does she?"

In the pile of garbage were photographs of Joel, fine clothing, and what looked like a collection of beer steins. Eddy was tempted to snag a few for himself, but he resisted. Tommy was right, it didn't seem like Anna had wasted any time discarding all of Joel's possessions. Perhaps she was just trying to put the tragedy behind her, but she hadn't even bothered to donate the good quality items.

"Do you know who she was seeing?" Eddy asked as he turned back to look at Tommy. Tommy was already gone. Eddy heard his front door slam shut. He thought about going up to the door and knocking, but he was fairly certain that he was not going to get anything else out of Tommy. He had a new lead to follow, but first he wanted to check in with Samantha.

Chapter Ten

When Eddy knocked on the door of Samantha's villa, he noticed something strange. The grass beside the front stoop had been trampled down. The rest of the lawn was perfectly manicured as usual. Eddy thought it was strange that only one patch was damaged. He was distracted by Samantha opening the front door.

"Hi Eddy, come in." She left the door open so that he could step inside and immediately walked over to her computer.

"Samantha, what happened by your front door?" Eddy asked.

"Huh? Nothing." Samantha shook her head. "I did some research on dear, old Abe." Samantha looked over at Eddy with a dark expression. "He is quite the con artist."

"What do you mean?" Eddy asked as he walked over to her. He rested one hand on the desk and peered at the screen. "What did you find?" He leaned closer to her.

"I found that he has been trying to get money out of many people one way or another. He has several lawsuits pending against several companies. Each one as frivolous as the last. It is as if he is waiting for one of them to pan out, no matter how outlandish the accusation is." She scrunched up her nose. "One of my pet peeves is using lawsuits to get rich."

"Well, that's not exactly criminal though." Eddy shrugged. "A lot of people try to get rich quick that way."

"Maybe, but he's also been accused of faking his disability." Samantha raised an eyebrow. "That does sound criminal to me."

"What?" Eddy's eyes widened. "How could he be faking it? He's in a wheelchair!"

"I know he is, you know he is, but how do we know he has to be in it? I could sit down in a wheelchair, too, and pretend not to be able to walk." Samantha tapped her finger lightly on the screen. "It says here that three years ago he was accused of fraud. However, the claim was never able to be proven."

"I know many people that have to fight to get their disability." Eddy frowned. "I don't think it's that unusual for people to have their application for it questioned."

"That may be true sometimes, but in Abe's case it went a step further than just suspicion. The disability lawyer was ready to bring a case against him. It wasn't just a denial, but an accusation of fraud. There's a big difference." She slid back in her chair so that Eddy could have a clearer view. "It doesn't say exactly why it was dismissed, just that it was unsubstantiated."

"Hmm. That is interesting. Maybe they couldn't prove it because there was no truth to it?" Eddy sighed. "I just can't imagine someone being able to fake that severe of an injury for so long. It's not like he's hobbling around on crutches."

"I don't think he could have faked it alone,"

Samantha agreed. "Which is likely why the lawyer couldn't prove fraud. He had all of the paperwork to back up his injuries."

"Did you find anything about the doctor who substantiated his injury?" Eddy asked eagerly.

"No, I can't access those details, but I know from an article I wrote that there are quite a few doctors out there who will diagnose anything if the price is right. I was wondering if you could try to find out who the doctor is," Samantha suggested. "What do you think?"

"Sure, I'll see what I can find out," he agreed. "Good idea, Samantha, I would have just left it because his injury was substantiated and thought it was a dead end."

"Well, it still may be." Samantha looked up at him. "Until we can confirm that Abe is truly faking his disability we have to assume that he is incapable of committing this murder. How did it go with Tommy?"

"Tommy." Eddy rolled his eyes. "I don't get the

urge to punch people too often, but that guy."

"Yes, I know. But what did he say about Doll?" Samantha was more than a little eager to find out if her suspicions had proven to be true.

"Samantha, let's not dirty this investigation with trite gossip." Eddy pursed his lips with distaste. Samantha was quietened by his attitude. She felt a little embarrassed for having asked. Then she saw that Eddy was trying not to grin.

"Eddy! Just tell me."

"Oh, he and Doll were definitely together. In fact he cut his hair to make sure that no one would recognize him when he was out on a date with her," Eddy lowered his voice. "Does that confirm things for you?"

"Yes, it does." Samantha shook her head with some wonder. "Isn't it odd how you can look at someone's life and think that it is absolutely perfect, then you find out about the dark secrets that don't show on the surface?"

"Samantha, no one has the perfect life. No

one," Eddy spoke with absolute confidence. Samantha knew that he was trying to reassure her, but his declaration actually saddened her. The thought that there wasn't a single person in the world living their fairy-tale, made her question the purpose of life. But it wasn't the right time to discuss their differing views.

"I guess you're right, at least in this case. So, now we can be fairly certain that Tommy didn't murder Joel. My gut is telling me we need to find out more about Abe." He narrowed his eyes. "Somehow he's involved in all of this. I'm going to call Walt and have him dig deeper into Abe's financials. I'll see if Chris can send over Abe's bank records so Walt can look through them."

"That's a good idea. If there's something there I know Walt will be able to find it. I'll ask him, and I'll do some research of my own as well. I just hope we can get to the bottom of this quickly. If Abe is involved he has the freedom to disappear." Samantha gritted her teeth. "I'm sure he thinks that no one is even considering him."

"I'm sure of that as well. I'm going to see if I can't find out a little more information about Abe's medical condition," Eddy sounded confident as he straightened his hat.

"How are you going to do that?" Samantha asked curiously. She knew that Eddy had his connections but she wasn't sure exactly who they were.

"I have my ways." Eddy winked lightly at her. "Let me know if Walt comes up with anything, all right?"

"Sure." Samantha nodded. Eddy began to walk towards the door. As soon as he touched the doorknob he remembered the way Samantha had sounded that morning. He stopped and turned back.

"Are you sure you're okay, Sam?" He looked across the room in an attempt to meet her eyes directly. "Nothing you want to tell me?"

"I'm fine." Samantha lowered her eyes shyly. She wasn't sure if she was really experiencing anything after all. She didn't want to advertise the fact that she might be getting a little forgetful, especially to Eddy, who would insist on her taking a back seat to the investigation if he thought it was too taxing for her.

"You know that you can tell me." Eddy hesitated. "I mean. We're friends, right?" He shifted uncomfortably and ended up sliding his hands into his pockets. Samantha eyed him with some confusion.

"Yes Eddy, of course we're friends." She nodded, but didn't offer any further information. She was entitled to her secrets.

"Well, then you should know that you don't have to hide things from me," Eddy repeated. "I guess I kind of come off a little gruff? I just want you to know, that if you need to talk, or you're worried about something, or anything..." he stumbled over his words. His voice trailed off as Samantha continued to stare at him.

"I know, Eddy." She smiled kindly at him. "I

appreciate it."

"All right." He looked like he might say more, or maybe he expected her to say more. When Samantha replied only with silence Eddy nodded again and then stepped out the door.

Chapter Eleven

As Eddy was walking towards the Sage Garden's offices it was still bothering him that Samantha wasn't being completely honest with him. It wasn't the deceit that bothered him, but the fact that she felt she couldn't be honest with him. He was caught up in what the reason might be, when he reached the front office of Sage Gardens.

"Eddy!" Owen's voice carried from the door of his smaller medical office. He stepped all the way outside to greet Eddy.

"Just who I was looking for." Eddy walked up to Owen with a broad smile. He could see that Owen had been studying as he had a pencil tucked behind his ear and an exhausted look on his face. Eddy knew that Owen was working towards becoming a doctor so he stole every minute he could between the patients he saw at Sage Gardens.

"Uh oh, am I in trouble?" Owen asked. He smiled warmly, showing that he wasn't actually concerned.

"No, not in trouble. But I was hoping to get a minute of your time. If you're not too busy." He pointed out the pencil behind Owen's ear.

"Sure, I could use a break. How are you doing, Eddy?" Owen nodded towards the office where two uniformed officers were questioning some of the security staff. "Are you holding up okay with all of this? I still can't believe that Joel is gone. And murder?" Owen lowered his voice. "Are you getting in the middle of all of this, Eddy?"

"I'm doing all right. Yes, you could say that I am getting involved. We're trying to get to the bottom of a few things, and I was hoping to pick your brain a bit." Eddy nodded. He gestured to a wooden bench beneath a shade tree. "Can we sit?"

"Sure." Owen sat down beside Eddy with a look of concern. "What can I help you with?"

"I've got a delicate question to ask you." Eddy cleared his throat. He knew that he was pushing the boundaries of his friendship with Owen. "I'd rather it was kept between you and me."

"Oh sure, Eddy, I can get you a prescription for that, it happens to most men as they get older, it's nothing that should cause you any shame." He reached into his pocket to pull out his cell phone. "I can set you up with a good doctor to get checked out. When are you available?"

"What?" Eddy blinked. "What would I need a doctor for?"

Owen looked up at him with a faint blush in his cheeks. Eddy stared at him for a moment. Suddenly he figured out what Owen was thinking. "No, that's not what I meant, Owen. Unbelievable." He shook his head.

"Oh." Owen's eyes widened. "I'm sorry, it's just that I get asked for it a lot and you said the question was delicate."

"It's not about me, it's about someone else."

Eddy briefly glowered at Owen and then focused on the information he needed. "It's about Abe."

"Abe?" Owen grimaced with recognition of the name. "What about him?"

"I figured since he is wheelchair-bound that you probably see him pretty often. Is that so?" Eddy knew that Owen was primarily hired to see the patients at Sage Gardens that needed a little more focused care.

"You're right, I am supposed to see him." Owen's expression was grim. "Abe is one of my troublemakers."

"What do you mean?" Eddy leaned in with interest. Owen was the friendly type, and it wasn't often that Eddy saw him get frustrated with anyone.

"I mean I schedule him appoints with me, and also with the physical therapist that he is supposed to see, and he always cancels or is unreachable. I've even gone to his villa before for a home visit to make sure that he has everything he needs and he refused to let me in. It's very frustrating. It's not just about the paperwork either. I'm concerned about him." Owen's eyes widened with hope. "Do you think that you might be able to talk to him for me? See if you can get him to come into the office? It's for his own good."

"I don't think so." Eddy shook his head. He thumped his knee with his fist. "I think he has a very good reason for not showing up at your office."

"What reason?" Owen frowned. "I'd give him excellent care," his voice held a hint of defensiveness.

"Oh, I know you would." Eddy met Owen's eyes with a sincere smile. "That's not the problem. The problem is that I don't think Abe needs any medical care at all. At least not the kind that you have in mind."

"You've lost me." Owen looked confused. "Is this some kind of riddle?" He wiped his hands across his face.

"No. I wish it was a joke. I'm fairly certain that Abe is faking his need for that wheelchair." Eddy grimaced at the very idea. The leaves in the tree above him fluttered with the faint breeze. He could hear in the distance the sounds of the ducks splashing in the pond. He was sure that everything about Sage Gardens was about to be tainted with what he had to say. It was meant to be a peaceful, safe place for people to grow old with dignity. A place where neighbors could trust one another. Not a place where neighbors were deceitful.

"Eddy, that is a terrible thing to suggest," Owen spoke cautiously. Eddy could tell that he was not accusing him of anything. Owen was just shocked by the idea. "Are you sure?" Owen asked.

"I'm not sure. But I suspect it very strongly. In fact, I suspect that Abe might be a suspect in Joel Westons' death." He sighed heavily. "It's not that I want it to be true, Owen, believe me. But I think the facts are adding up to point in that direction."

"It's impossible." Owen shook his head firmly. "I would know if he was faking it."

"Would you?" Eddy raised an eyebrow and met Owen's eyes. "Owen, if Abe is faking his condition he is a seasoned and skilled con artist. He's had me fooled. What makes you think he couldn't fool you?"

"Well, I just don't see how I wouldn't have noticed." Owen appeared mystified. Eddy knew that he was doing the same thing that Eddy himself had done when he first thought of the idea. Owen was sorting through his memories for any hint that Abe could have been faking.

"Have you ever actually examined his legs?" Eddy asked gently. He didn't want Owen to feel as if he was questioning his skills as a nurse, or interrogating him. But Eddy needed Owen to give him as much information as possible, and fast.

"No. I've examined other things about him. But there was never a reason for me to examine his legs. The physical therapist is supposed to let me know if there is a problem," Owen's voice trailed off with disbelief.

"The physical therapist that Abe has refused to see, right?" Eddy waited for Owen to come to the same conclusion that he had.

"Right." Owen stared hard across the circular drive of the entrance of Sage Gardens. The tall grass surrounding the pond waved slowly back and forth in the faint wind. Eddy sat back against the bench. He waited while Owen processed the realization that Eddy might just be right. "Could it be possible?" Owen asked finally. "That he could have fooled all of us, all of this time?"

"I think stranger things have happened. I've always seen Abe as a pretty private person. I don't think that's terribly abnormal. But now that I think back I can see that he is extremely private. He never accepted help from anyone, which I always assumed was just him being stubborn, but now I see that it was probably a way of preventing anyone from getting too close." He stood up from the bench and turned to look down at Owen. "Is it possible that I'm letting my imagination run away from me? I suppose it is. But my hunches rarely fail me."

"What can I do to help?" Owen asked.

"We need to get access to Abe's medical records. They are not easy to obtain." Eddy slid his hands into his pockets. He knew that what he was asking Owen for was no simple task. If Owen violated confidentiality he could lose his job and even face legal charges. During their friendship, Eddy had yet to have to ask Owen to do anything illegal. Now, this would be a true test of their friendship.

"You know I can't do that, Eddy," Owen's tone grew dark. "I would do anything to help you, Eddy, but that's crossing a line."

"I know it is, Owen." Eddy scowled and lifted his gaze past the younger man for a moment. He knew that he could convince Owen if he really tried. But it left him conflicted to even consider it.

"What would you need to know?" Owen

asked. When Eddy looked back at Owen, the younger man refused to look directly at him.

"The name of the doctor that diagnosed him and more information about him if possible. I also think finding out what his official injury was, and the cause would be useful." Eddy sat back down on the edge of the bench beside Owen. "Listen, Owen I hate to put you in this position, but I'm about to ask my friends to risk a lot to find out the truth about Abe. I'd like to know a little more about him before I do that. Do you understand?"

"I do." Owen continued to stare hard at the perfectly manicured grass beneath his feet. His short, blonde hair caught the sunlight. Eddy was reminded of just how young he was.

"You know what, never mind. Forget I asked." Eddy stood up quickly from the bench. "I never should have asked you, Owen, I'm sorry for that."

"Wait Eddy, just let me think about it." Owen looked up at him with surprise.

"No." Eddy met his eyes sternly. "I never

should have asked you. Put it out of your head. I have other ways I can get the information."

"But I could…"

"No," Eddy repeated, even more gruffly. "You're a good man, Owen, and no one gets to change that about you, especially not me."

As Eddy walked away he felt terrible for even having asked Owen in the first place. He had let his desire to solve the case take over his better judgement, just like old times. There was more than one occasion in the past where he had bent the law and even broken it because he became so obsessed about finding the truth. Retirement was supposed to allow him to put all of that behind him. So far all it had done was give him too much time on his hands. When he glanced back over his shoulder, Owen was no longer on the bench. Eddy could only hope that his request hadn't damaged their friendship. The time he spent with Owen discussing old cases and life in general was very valuable to him.

Chapter Twelve

Walt had just hung up from a phone call with Samantha where she had asked him to look into Abe's financial history and she had explained that they were suspicious that Abe was faking his injuries. Walt found this information more than a little troubling. The idea that Abe might really be faking his injury left a bad taste in his mouth. He had just begun digging into Abe's financials when he heard the screen door on his porch swing open.

"Hi Walt!" Jo stuck her head inside the door.

"Jo, hello. I wasn't expecting you." He smiled as he turned to face her. "Come in, please."

"Sorry to just drop in, but I wanted to see what is happening with the murder investigation and I was hoping Samantha would be here as I tried calling her and Eddy, but they're not answering." She stepped into the villa.

"Oh yes, Samantha called me a little while

ago. She suspects Abe might be faking his injuries," Walt explained.

"Wow!" Jo gasped.

"She asked me to look into Abe's financials." He gestured to the computer. "So, that's what I've been doing. She'll be coming over soon."

"Oh good. Then you don't mind if I stay?" Jo plopped down on Walt's couch.

"Of course not. In fact, I'd like your opinion on something." He turned in his office chair to fully face her.

"What is it?" Jo asked. She brushed her long, dark hair back over her shoulders and looked at him intently. She knew that if it was a question that Walt couldn't answer himself it had to be interesting.

"Did you know many con artists in your," he hesitated for a moment, "previous career?"

Jo smiled at the delicate way he posed the question. "Yes, I've had the luxury of knowing quite a few actually," her voice carried sarcasm, but Walt didn't seem to catch it.

"Luxury?" he repeated.

"It was a joke," Jo pointed out. "I have known many con artists, yes."

"Do you think that someone could pull off faking such a severe impairment that we suspect Abe has been doing for so long?" Walt asked.

Jo thought about it for a moment. She took a breath and then nodded. "The key to being a good con artist, is to not be a con artist."

"Come again?" Walt asked. He blinked with confusion.

"If you want to pull off a con, especially one this involved, you have to become the role. If Abe really is faking it, he probably barely remembers that he's pretending. He's going to live his life as if the injury is real, all of the time, so that he tricks his own mind into instinctively believing that it was true. When someone is that dedicated, it's nearly impossible to see through the ruse." Jo gazed at Walt with fascination. "I guess not impossible for

Abe if it turns out to be true."

"I find it absolutely impossible to believe that someone could live for so long telling so many lies." Walt shook his head. "I just don't understand how someone could be so deceitful."

"Be glad that you don't," Jo's voice was quiet as she looked at him. "It's a good thing that you can't imagine it."

"I suppose it is." Walt turned back to the computer and continued with his research.

***

Samantha headed out to meet up with Walt. As she was locking her door, she ran through a checklist in her mind. Had she closed and locked all of the windows? Yes. Had she locked the back door? Yes. The villa should be secure. She started to walk down her driveway when something made her pause. In the soil between the walkway and the driveway there was an odd track. It reminded her of the track she had seen beside the picnic bench the day before. Her heart lurched as she realized that whatever made that track, and the track by her villa, might have been in the possession of the killer.

Samantha decided to check out the area beneath the kitchen window and the bedroom window. As she walked around behind the villa she searched the ground for any signs of the same tracks. She didn't see anything until she reached her kitchen window. Then she saw the same tracks right below the window. Her stomach twisted with fear. She had been ignoring her suspicions that someone might have been inside her villa, but now it was looking more and more like a reality.

Samantha shivered at the thought that she hadn't even bothered to notify the police. She walked to her bedroom window. As she suspected there were more tracks outside her bedroom window. She crouched down to take a closer look. They were more like grooves than tracks. She started to stand back up.

"What are you doing?"

Samantha shrieked before she had the chance to recognize the voice. Once she realized that it was Eddy it was too late, she had already spun around with her fists in the air.

"Samantha!" Eddy looked at her with more concern than anger. "What is going on? Are you ready to tell me the truth now?"

Samantha felt hesitant as she looked into his eyes. She hated to seem fearful in front of Eddy, who seemed never to be afraid of anything.

"I think someone has been breaking into my villa," she admitted.

"Why didn't you tell me about this?" Eddy admonished. "Samantha, this is serious."

"I know it's serious. Well, actually I didn't." She sighed. "I thought maybe it was all my imagination. I kept finding windows open, and I just assumed that I was forgetting to close them."

"Samantha, I know you better than that. You

have great instincts," he said. "You just didn't want to tell me."

"I just wanted to be sure. I'm still not sure." She looked back at the grooves in the grass. "I found these tracks by the front door, and by the kitchen window as well. I'm not sure what could have made them. But I think they look similar to the ones we saw by the picnic bench, remember?"

"Where we thought the killer might have been watching Joel's villa." Eddy nodded. "I remember. They do look the same." He peered even closer. As Samantha watched Eddy run his fingers along the grooves she suddenly had an idea of what they might be.

"Wheelchair tracks!" She cried out with such enthusiasm that Eddy jumped at the sudden sound.

"Huh?" He looked back down at the ground. "I think you're right about that. It looks as if the wheels on Abe's chair could have easily made these marks."

"That would explain why there are no footprints anywhere," Samantha growled. "He probably just rolled right up to the window and stood up on the seat. That would give him easy access to the windows. Unbelievable." She shuddered at the thought of Abe being in her home when she wasn't there, or even possibly when she was.

"But why?" Eddy asked. "Why would Abe, if he really is faking his injury, be climbing in your windows?"

"I think he was trying to scare me," Samantha replied thoughtfully. "I think he was hoping that I would get frightened and stop looking into this case. Or maybe he suspected that I had information or evidence inside."

"Maybe." Eddy nodded. He swept his gaze along the paths around Samantha's villa.

"Maybe you should stay with Jo until we get all of this settled," he suggested as he looked back towards Samantha. "Just to be safe."

Samantha looked uncertain. She didn't want to admit to being terrified, but she was. However, she also wasn't sure whether Jo would welcome a house guest. She was an extremely private person.

"I have a better idea. Why don't we get this solved?" She looked at Eddy with determination.

"That is a better idea," Eddy agreed. "Let's go see what Walt's found."

***

When Samantha and Eddy arrived at Walt's villa, Samantha was surprised to see Jo sprawled across his couch. She had a few papers in her hands that she appeared to be reading over.

"What have you found?" Eddy asked as he stepped up behind Walt.

"Some very interesting information about our

friend Abe," Walt replied.

"What is it?" Eddy pressed.

Jo sat up on the couch to make room for Samantha to sit.

"You okay?" she asked. She noticed the tension in Samantha's face.

"I will be when we have all of this settled."

"Well, it looks to me that Abe was paying Joel money on a monthly basis," Walt explained. "It is paid into Joel's personal account so I didn't see it before and I assume it isn't an investment in one of Joel's businesses. It was a payment of a small amount, not enough for it to be an investment, and not so little that it didn't have a purpose."

"What do you think it was for?" Eddy asked with growing interest.

"I honestly don't know. But I'll look into it more. I want to find out what it's for."

"All right, well let's focus on Abe. Samantha, could you do some more research maybe into whether there is a deeper link between Abe and

Tommy, or Abe and one of Joel's other clients? Somehow he's connected to all of this, and I want to know how," Eddy spoke with determination.

"What about what we were considering?" Samantha asked. "Is Abe faking his disability?"

"I've got nothing to prove that in his financial records." Walt frowned. "There's no evidence of him visiting any place that would require him to be capable of walking. He has purchased all of his medical needs on a regular basis, so there's no sign that he wasn't using them."

"Well, if the answer isn't in his finances, then maybe we need to look more deeply somewhere else," Jo suggested.

"That's true." Eddy stood up and paced through the living room. "We need to find some proof that he is not bound to that wheelchair before we can make any kind of accusation."

"How can we do that?" Walt wondered.

"People usually hide their secrets in their homes," Eddy pointed out grimly. "I can't tell you how many times I've uncovered the deepest secrets just by looking under someone's mattress."

"Maybe we could just try and pay him a friendly visit," Walt suggested.

"That won't work. He doesn't invite people into his home," Eddy explained.

"Which makes him all the more suspicious," Samantha stated.

"So, we break in?" Eddy looked a little uncomfortable.

"I could help with that." Jo smiled faintly. She could tell that it was what everyone wanted, but was afraid to ask for. Normally, she would have been hesitant, but in this case, she was determined. "I can't stand the idea of someone faking a disability. I'm not convinced that Abe is, but trust me I've known plenty of people that knew how to perform a great con."

"So, maybe if we sneak into Abe's villa we could find out if he actually needs that wheelchair." Eddy slapped his palm lightly on the table top. "Then we'll know whether he is a suspect or not."

Samantha cringed at the idea. "What if we don't find anything? Or worse, what if we're caught? What explanation could we give for being in a disabled man's home in the middle of the night?"

"Don't worry about that. I won't get caught." Jo offered a confident smile. "I only need a little time to get prepared. So, maybe a bit later tonight, provided that Abe is not at home? Does that sound good?"

"Perfect." Eddy nodded.

"You're sure?" Samantha asked. "I don't want you to feel like you have to, Jo."

"I know I don't have to. I think I know you well enough now, Samantha. I know that you'd only suggest it if it was for a good cause. So, maybe my past is checkered, but now I can use my skills for good." She lifted her eyes to Eddy. "As long as you recognize that you're just as involved as me."

"Excuse me?" Eddy leaned forward slightly. "What exactly are you suggesting?"

"I'm suggesting that I need to know I'm not the only one at risk here. If I was to be caught, I would not be the only one. Understand?" She raised an eyebrow.

"Is that a threat?" Eddy looked at her with widened eyes.

"It's not," Jo's voice softened. "I only meant that if we are going to work as a team, then we take the risk as a team. I feel like you three get together and investigate, but I am left on the sidelines until you need something unsavory done. I don't mind the unsavory part, but if I'm going to put myself on the line, I want to know that the rest of you are as well."

"That sounds reasonable." Samantha nodded. "Can we all agree?"

The others all nodded. Jo smiled with relief.

"Then I'll take care of it right away. See if you

can distract Abe long enough. I won't need more than a half hour. Okay?" She stood up and walked towards the door.

"Jo, be careful," Walt called out before she could disappear through the door.

"I will be," she promised.

Chapter Thirteen

After gathering a few items she always used for a break-in, Jo headed to Abe's villa. Samantha had texted her that she and Eddy were keeping an eye on Abe who was engaged in a card game at the recreation center. Jo knew that Samantha would text her the moment that changed. As she reached Abe's villa she checked for anyone nearby. No one seemed to be out and about walking.

Jo made her way casually around the side of his villa as if she had a reason to be there. She used her tools to release the lock on the kitchen door. She held her breath as the lock clicked. Once more she looked around to see if anyone was in sight. When she was sure the coast was clear she slipped in through the kitchen door.

The kitchen was spotless. Jo searched it as she moved through it. Everything in the kitchen had been modified for wheelchair access. The counters were lower. The appliances were spaced so that Abe would have room to turn around when needed. In the corner of the kitchen there was a small pile of towels and wash cloths. Jo assumed they were for the laundry. It would make sense for Abe to pile them there instead of wheeling into the laundry room which had a narrow entrance. This was one of the small things that Jo was looking for to confirm Abe's disability. If in the comfort of his own home he didn't get up out of the chair to toss the laundry in the washer, then it was pretty safe to say that he was probably not faking.

Still, Jo wanted more of a confirmation. She made her way through the empty living room. When she reached the short hallway that led to the bedroom she hesitated for a moment. She was entering very personal space. If there was going to be proof of Abe faking his injury, she might find it in the bathroom or bedroom. As she moved silently down the hallway she noticed that the bathroom door was slightly open. She paused to peek inside. Just as she had expected, the shower and bath tub had been modified for Abe's use. The sink was also lower and there was enough room in the bathroom for Abe to roll in and back out. It was clear to Jo that the bathroom was being used by someone who needed extra assistance. She sighed as she knew that all of this information might blow Eddy's theory.

Jo headed to the bedroom for the last part of her investigation. The bedroom door was wide open. She inched her way down the hallway. As she peered around the door she saw that the bedroom was empty. She assumed it would be, but she was always cautious. In the bedroom she saw that the bed was untidy. On the nightstand were a few prescription pill bottles. She picked them up and looked them over. Nothing seemed out of the ordinary to her. She set them back down in the exact same spot. She walked over to the closet and took a look inside the door which was slightly open. Again, everything was positioned within reach of someone who was in a wheelchair.

Jo began to feel guilty for invading Abe's privacy. If their suspicions were wrong, then she had just broken into an innocent man's home. She felt a strong desire to leave. With one more quick glance over the room she shook her head. There was nothing to find. She made her way back through the house and back out of the kitchen door. As soon as she was a safe distance from Abe's villa she texted Samantha.

It's clean, there's no proof. I think we might have been wrong.

Samantha looked down at the text that came through on her phone. Then she looked up at Abe who was winning at a hand of cards. He seemed comfortable in his wheelchair. If Jo hadn't found any proof of him faking his need for the chair, then maybe they really had been wrong.

"What is it?" Eddy asked.

"Nothing," Samantha said. "She didn't find

anything."

"Are you sure?" Eddy was perplexed. He was certain that Jo would find something.

"Trust me, if Jo said there was nothing, there was nothing. You know how good she is at what she does."

"Used to do," Eddy corrected.

"Right." Samantha frowned. "I'm sorry, Eddy. Maybe we need to rethink things."

"Maybe." Eddy sighed. "I'm going to head to my place. I have a few more contacts I can reach out to."

"Okay," Samantha replied. She decided to linger long enough to watch the end of the game. She felt a little silly for suspecting that Abe had somehow been able to break into her villa and Joel's villa through a window, and commit murder. He was just a man, playing cards, and grieving for a friend.

***

Eddy walked towards his villa with his mind on Jo's break-in. Without any evidence to prove that Abe was faking his disability, they weren't going to get very far with him as a suspect. Eddy was almost at his villa when Owen came jogging up behind him.

"Eddy, wait a minute!" He called out. Eddy stopped and turned to face him.

"Owen." He was too troubled by the case to smile.

Owen was a little out of breath as if he had been trying to catch up with Eddy for some time. "Listen, I have something to tell you."

"What?" Eddy paused outside his villa. "Do you want to come inside?"

"That might be best," Owen agreed. Eddy opened the door for him. Though Eddy and Owen had been getting close since Eddy had moved in, Eddy had yet to have Owen inside his villa.

"A drink?" Eddy offered.

"No, thank you." Owen looked uncomfortable as he glanced around Eddy's sparsely decorated living room. There was one very old easy chair positioned in front of the television, while the other furniture in the room appeared to be untouched. "I did what you asked."

"What did I ask?" Eddy studied him.

"I looked into Abe's medical history."

Eddy was silenced by Owen's admission. He hadn't really expected Owen to go through with it. The fact that he did, meant a lot to Eddy. "And?" he asked.

"And, you were right to be suspicious. The doctor that both diagnosed and treated Abe has been involved in many disability cases and has a bad reputation for fraud cases. He has even faced jail time in the past, but managed to get out of it. I am surprised that he still has a license. I'm not saying that Abe's injury is fake, but knowing who his doctor is and the doctor's history, I would be more inclined to believe it." Owen looked downhearted. "I can't believe that he pulled the wool over my eyes for so long. When you first suggested it I thought it was impossible. Now, I see that it could very well be true. Unfortunately, the doctor's criminal history is privileged, it's not going to help out in the investigation."

"Maybe not." Eddy narrowed his eyes. "But it does make Abe the primary suspect. If he's lying about his injury then he is probably capable of killing Joel. I'm not going to let him get away with it."

"What are you going to do?" Owen asked. "Eddy, I don't want to see you get into trouble over all of this."

"Don't worry about that, Owen. Thank you for getting the information, I really appreciate it. You can be certain that I will keep your name out of this." He grimaced. "Now, if you'll excuse me, I have some work to do."

Owen nodded and reluctantly turned to leave. Eddy could tell that he wanted to advise him not to get involved. But Owen knew Eddy well enough to know better than to bother with that.

Chapter Fourteen

Eddy called everyone together at Walt's villa to discuss the information that Owen had shared with him. His friends looked at him expectantly.

"I spoke to my contacts, and it turns out that the doctor Abe used to qualify for disability has had several complaints against him. In fact he's had accusations of fraud. None that could be substantiated."

"I think there might be some proof that Abe was faking it if you look at his financial transactions." Walt slapped a few papers down on the table between them. "I suspect that the weekly payments from Abe to Joel were for something devious."

"What are they?" Eddy asked.

"Well, the more I thought about the payments, the more I realized how unlikely they were," Walt stated. "Abe might be a fraud, but he's not stupid. So, I looked into it a little more. Abe was paying weekly instalments to Joel's checking account. Joel didn't shift that money to any business account."

"So, what were the payments for?" Samantha asked again. She couldn't imagine what Abe would be paying Joel for.

"I've seen these types of payments before. They were almost always for the purpose of blackmail or extortion," Walt said confidently.

"You think that Joel was blackmailing Abe?" Eddy looked confused for a moment and then snapped his fingers. "Because Joel found out that Abe could walk!"

"Exactly," Walt confirmed. "Or at least that's my theory. I think that Joel found out somehow, and Abe agreed to make payments to him to keep his silence. But I don't think Abe really had the income to support that, so he might have just decided to reduce his spending."

"That's a very cold way of putting it," Samantha said

"It's all checks and balances, Samantha." Walt shook his head. "To think that Abe would go so far as to murder someone to protect his con, it's a terrible thing, but the money doesn't lie."

"We still don't know for sure though. How are we going to get him to admit to it?" Samantha sighed as she tried to sort through ideas in her mind. "If we accuse him and then he finds a way to convince people that he is disabled, we will look horrible."

"We need proof," Jo agreed. "Solid proof."

"But you didn't find anything in his villa." Samantha shrugged. "Could it just be a coincidence?"

"That or he's a very skilled con artist." Jo frowned. "Maybe I missed something."

"No matter what we need to find a way to prove it." Eddy looked between his friends. "We need to know for sure."

"Maybe if we give him a reason to get up and walk." Samantha smiled faintly. "If he murdered

Joel he was motivated enough to get up out of the chair. So we just have to come up with something that will inspire him to do it again."

"We could make him believe we're about to find out the truth," Jo suggested. "A con artist will go to any length to hide their con."

"Sage Gardens is hosting a memorial for Joel this afternoon. I heard about it at the recreation center. I'm sure that Abe will be there. It would be the perfect time to set the trap." Samantha's expression had a wicked edge. "I want to know if he has been breaking into my villa."

"Me too," Eddy's voice was dark.

"Then it's settled." Walt nodded. "We'll set the trap at the memorial this afternoon. If Abe thinks we have something good on him from Joel's financial records then he might just take a risk and get out of his chair. If we catch him in the act he might be shocked enough to confess to the murder."

"We can set the trap for my place," Samantha

declared. "He seems pretty familiar with how to get in there."

"No," Eddy and Walt both spoke up at the same time.

Samantha narrowed her eyes. "And just why not?"

"They're right, Samantha." Jo drew the attention of all three at the table.

"They are?" Samantha asked with surprise.

"We are?" Eddy muttered with mirrored confusion.

"Not for the reasons you're thinking." Jo rolled her eyes. "Eddy, Abe knows you and Walt well enough to know that you would never leave crucial evidence in Samantha's villa. It would put her at risk. He'll smell a trap. Besides, if we're going to trap him with Joel's financial records it's going to make more sense for that information to be at Walt's house. So, although I'm sure that Samantha is perfectly capable of protecting herself, it wouldn't be a good plan to set the trap in her villa."

"I guess Jo is right, just remember what she said boys, perfectly capable of protecting myself." Samantha lifted her chin with a touch of pride. Eddy met her eyes and lifted an eyebrow just slightly.

"So, how did Abe get your windows open? Weren't they locked?"

Everyone else at the table fell silent as they waited for Samantha to answer.

"Probably," she shot back. "I mean, I thought they were."

"It's easy to get complacent in a place like this," Walt spoke with warning in his voice. "But even the safest of neighborhoods can be dangerous. Statistically speaking, most home invaders will walk away if they find a locked door or window. They want an easy target, and won't take the risk of having to drill through or break glass."

"Even a locked window can be unlocked if you

know how," Jo said knowingly. They all looked at her but didn't question her further.

"So, maybe I should come check your windows for you?" Eddy suggested. "See if we can make them more secure."

"I'm sure I can handle it." Samantha looked pointedly at Eddy. "Thank you, Walt, for that good reminder. Now, what about this trap we're setting? It's going to be at Walt's?"

"I guess it would be best." Walt looked nervous as he stared down at the top of the table. Samantha was sure that he was not used to having people in his own space. He invited people over, but having someone invade his home was a different story.

"Don't worry, Walt, we'll make sure the situation is monitored," Samantha assured him.

"I think that we should have someone other than Walt in his home for the night," Jo added. "Just in case things don't go exactly as planned."

"I will be close by to take him down." Eddy

leaned forward slightly. "If he sees me he'll flee. So, I will be watching from the outside."

"Then I'll be inside." Jo nodded. "We can always put up some cameras to record Abe out of his chair. That way no one can argue the truth."

"What about me?" Samantha asked. "I could hide in the closet in Walt's room."

"What are you going to do if something goes wrong?" Jo asked. She offered a grimace of concern. "Samantha, Abe is a murderer."

"And he's been breaking into my house. Trust me, I want him to go down. Besides, I can handle myself." She cleared her throat. Jo met Samantha's eyes. The two women seemed to exchange some kind of understanding.

"All right. If Samantha says that she can handle it, then I trust her." Jo looked between the two men. "Anybody have a problem with that?"

Walt and Eddy looked at each other and then back at Samantha. "No problem," Eddy agreed.

"Okay, so Samantha will be in the closet, Walt

will be in the bed, and Eddy and I will be outside."
Jo smiled at Eddy. "Do you think you can handle my company on a stakeout?"

"I might be able to tolerate it." Eddy offered an indifferent expression.

Samantha tried not to smile. "So, it's a plan. What time are we going to meet?"

"I'm thinking after eight. That way it's early enough that Abe shouldn't already be staking out the house, and late enough that it's believable that Walt will be in bed." Eddy tilted his head towards Walt. "Does that work for you?"

"Sure, I am in bed by eight fifty every night. That gives me ten minutes to fall asleep, so that I am asleep by exactly nine."

Jo raised an eyebrow.

"I think that's great that you make your health a priority, Walt. Everyone knows sleep is the most crucial key to your wellbeing." Samantha smiled.

With the plan settled the friends parted ways. They each had their role to fill and none of it would

179

work if Abe suspected any of them.

Chapter Fifteen

When the time came for the memorial, Samantha walked towards the gathering. She could see that most of her friends and neighbors were already there. Sage Gardens treated death like a social occasion in many ways. There was always plenty of company, plenty of food, and plenty of alcohol. The square in the center of Sage Gardens was the meeting place for most events if the weather was nice, otherwise the recreation hall was used.

Since it was a sunny and clear afternoon the square had been filled with lawn chairs, portable tables, and some umbrellas. Samantha noticed that a few of the residents had brought out their instruments to contribute to the memorial. It was a beautiful sight, but it occurred to Samantha that many of these people probably didn't like Joel. If they found out the whole truth about him, she was sure that they wouldn't like him.

"Samantha, hello." Walt stepped up beside her and caught her elbow gently with his palm. "We're over here." He gestured to one of the shaded picnic tables. Samantha saw that Eddy was already seated at the table with a beer bottle in his hand.

"Where's Jo?" Samantha asked. She knew full well that Jo was setting up cameras in Walt's house, but she didn't want anyone at the memorial to wonder why the three of them were together without their fourth friend. She walked with Walt towards the table.

"Oh, you know Jo, she's more of a loner than a joiner," Walt said. "She said something about taking a nap." He lowered his voice as they got closer to the gathering, "Eddy is already playing his role, so just be warned." He furrowed an eyebrow.

Samantha felt herself tense slightly. She knew that this wasn't about being social. They all had to be careful not to tip off Abe in any way. The thought of the man made her look for him. She searched through the faces in the crowd. She didn't see Abe anywhere. She did see Cynthia Doll and her husband, standing beside a huge wreath of flowers that were dedicated to Joel.

Anna was sitting in a chair beside the wreath with a box of tissues on one knee and a plate of food on the other. She looked like she had been crying, but it could have been allergies from all of the pollen in the air. Samantha felt a pang of guilt for suspecting Anna in the first place. Whether or not she and Joel had been in love, she had still lost her husband to the hands of a ruthless murderer. Samantha and her friends had considered her a suspect instead of the victim that she clearly was. Samantha thought about going over to her to offer her condolences again, but she didn't want to get too close to Cynthia. She might end up saying the wrong thing. Cynthia seemed to be avoiding looking in Samantha's direction as well.

Tommy was nowhere to be seen. Samantha imagined he had made himself scarce since

Cynthia's husband was there. As she sat down at the picnic table, Eddy looked over at her. His eyes were rimmed red and his cheeks were flushed. He spoke loudly, directly into her face.

"Samantha! So good of you to come!" He leaned close and planted a sloppy wet kiss on her cheek. Samantha drew back in horror and grabbed a napkin.

"Eddy!" Samantha scolded him as she wiped her cheek clean.

"What?" Eddy slurred his words as he spoke. "I'm just trying to have a good time. Don't be such a stick in the mud."

Samantha shot him a look of disbelief. She was honestly beginning to wonder if he was actually drunk instead of acting like it. Either way she was going to get him back for the slobber that he had left on her cheek. She shivered and crumpled up the napkin.

"Did you hear about it, Samantha?" Eddy asked, louder than he needed to. Walt handed

Eddy another beer.

"About what?" Samantha cleared her throat and remembered that she had a role to play.

"What really happened to our dear friend, Joel!" Eddy glanced around at the people that were close to him. "We know the truth now."

Samantha wondered why Eddy was putting on such a show when Abe wasn't even at the memorial yet. She assumed he was hoping that word would spread to Abe.

"What truth?" Samantha asked. She accepted a plate of food that Walt had put together for her.

As she looked up she saw that Abe was wheeling down the path towards the gathering. Abe's expression was as filled with grief as anyone would expect. He wheeled right over to Anna.

"Anna, I'm so sorry, again." Abe looked at her with a frown. "I know this is just a card, but I hope it means something." He held out an envelope to her. Anna refused to look directly at him. She

185

grabbed a tissue and dabbed at her eyes. "Just put it in the pile please." She gestured to the pile of cards and flowers on the table beside her.

"Anna," Abe said. Samantha watched as he looked at her pleadingly. She wondered if Anna had her own suspicion about Abe and that was why she was acting so coldly to him.

"Just put it there, please," Anna hissed and looked pointedly away from him. Abe sighed and placed the card on the table. He turned his wheelchair around just in time for Eddy's next rant.

"I knew it! All along I knew it! That Joel was into some kind of illegal stuff." He shook his head. "No one could prove it. But my buddy here, can." He slapped Walt hard on the back.

Walt gulped and spilled some of his drink on his sweater. He shot a look of absolute hatred in Eddy's direction. Samantha jumped up and grabbed a napkin to dab away the liquid. Walt frowned and took the napkin from her.

"I'll do it," he grumbled. Samantha knew that he had to be furious. She gave Eddy a look of warning. Eddy pretended not to notice. He seemed to be very involved in playing his role.

"What are you talking about, Eddy?" Samantha asked through gritted teeth. "Are you going to get to the point or are you going to keep blathering on?"

"Watch it, woman." Eddy scowled at her. Samantha bit the tip of her tongue to keep from putting him directly in his place. She knew for certain that Eddy was taking full advantage of his opportunity to play drunk. He was going to regret it later, she would make sure of that. "The truth is that Joel's ledger is full of mysterious payments. As soon as Walt gets to the bottom of who was making these payments, the police will know who the killer is!"

"Eddy, this isn't the time or the place," Walt said reproachfully. Samantha was slightly impressed with his ability to be angry, but maybe the wine on his sweater helped make his acting more believable. She rarely had the chance to see him angry.

"Walt's got all of the information," Eddy boasted loudly. He knew that Abe was close enough to hear him. He took a swig of his beer to make it seem as if he was only being loud because of being a little drunk. "It's clear somebody was paying him money that didn't have to do with his business. I'm willing to bet that whoever was paying that money is the one who took Joel's life." He shook his head and slammed his beer bottle down on the table. "I'm going to make sure that Anna gets justice for what that animal did to her husband."

"All right, Eddy, just calm down," Samantha pleaded with him. "You're going to get everybody all upset."

"They should be upset," Eddy said in an angry tone. "Someone needs to stand up for what's right here. Joel might not have been perfect, but he was a husband. He had responsibilities to take care of, and he was doing just that. Nobody should be killed in their own living room. From behind no less," he muttered with disgust. "It takes a real coward to beat someone over the head when they don't even have the chance to defend themselves."

Samantha rubbed Eddy's back soothingly, as if she was trying to prevent him from exploding. "Eddy relax, the police will take care of it I'm sure."

"Not if I take care of it first." He took another swig of his beer. "When I figure out who did it, and from those financial records we will be able to, that person is going to pay dearly. I have no patience for a man who will kill someone over money."

Eddy was doing such a good job of sounding drunk and belligerent that a member of the security staff began walking towards them.

"Dial it back, Eddy," Samantha hissed under her breath. Eddy might not have heard her, or he might have just ignored her, either way he didn't dial anything back.

"Who's with me?" Eddy asked as he stood up from the picnic table. "Who's going to make sure the bastard who killed Joel doesn't get away with this?"

"Sir, you're going to have to sit down." The security officer fixed Eddy with a warning glare.

"That's what you would like, huh?" Eddy stared back at the security officer with equal sternness. "For all of us to just sit down? To just pretend that Joel never existed?"

"That's not the case at all. You're disrupting a memorial and making a nuisance in a public space. If you can't control yourself, I'm going to have to ask you to leave."

The officer took a step closer to Eddy. Samantha rolled her eyes. She knew that Eddy was just pretending, but no one else did. It seemed to her that Eddy was putting on far too much of a show.

"I'm not going anywhere. I pay to live here," Eddy snarled and tossed his beer bottle down between himself and the officer. Luckily it was empty, or beer would have spilled all over the man's shoes.

"That's it!" The officer grabbed Eddy's arm.

"Eddy!" Samantha cried out with exasperation. "Cut it out!" She looked into his eyes. Eddy offered her a nearly imperceptible wink. His lips were twitching, she realized not with anger, but with an attempt to hold back his laughter.

Before the officer could haul Eddy away Owen came jogging over. "What's going on here?" he asked. "Let go of him!"

"He's drunk," the officer stated flatly. He continued to hold onto Eddy's arm.

"He lost a friend." Owen stared hard at the security officer. "Just let go of him."

The officer reluctantly let go of Eddy's arm. "This is on you, Owen. You need to get him somewhere to sober up. Understand?"

"I do." Owen nodded and continued to stand

close to Eddy. Samantha sighed and shook her head shamefully.

"You'll see," Eddy barked out. "Walt has the best mind for money around. He'll find the truth, and then whoever did this to Joel and Anna is going to pay!"

"Eddy, enough," Owen said through gritted teeth. "Please, come with me."

Eddy staggered a bit as if he was about to lose his balance. He leaned heavily on Owen's arm. Owen guided him down the path towards Eddy's villa. Once they were a good distance from the memorial Eddy straightened up.

"Eddy, what are you thinking? I've never known you to drink this much." Owen frowned.

"I'm not drunk, Owen." Eddy shook his head.

"There's no point in denying it, Eddy. If you have a problem, I can get you help."

"I'm not drunk, Owen!" Eddy repeated with exasperation. "I was faking it."

"Why would you do that?" Owen stared at

him. He squinted his eyes as if he was trying to tell for sure whether Eddy was drunk or not.

"Because I wanted someone to overhear something, and I didn't want to just blurt it out randomly. Drunk people say anything, so I had a good excuse for blathering on." Eddy patted Owen lightly on the back. "But I appreciate you having my back, Owen. Don't think I didn't notice that."

"You almost got yourself arrested." Owen shook his head with displeasure. "I'm sure there was another way you could have gotten your point across."

"Maybe." Eddy flashed him a grin. "But it wouldn't have been nearly as much fun."

Owen looked at him with a stern expression. "Whatever you're doing, just be careful."

"I will," Eddy assured him. Then he walked away. He sent a text to Jo to check on the progress with the cameras. She texted back right away.

Everything is in place. See you at eight.

Eddy smiled inwardly. He saw Samantha walking towards her villa. In the distance he caught sight of Walt nearing his villa. He was still scrubbing at his sweater. Everything was falling into place. Eddy could only hope that the evening would go as smoothly.

Chapter Sixteen

At eight o'clock on the dot Samantha knocked on Walt's side door. They were doing their best to keep their arrival under wraps. Walt opened the door almost right away.

"Hi Samantha," he said with a smile. Samantha noticed he had on crisp pajamas and his hair was perfectly combed. He pushed his glasses up slightly on his nose. "Come in quickly before anyone sees."

Samantha wasn't sure if he was more worried about Abe spotting her or a nosy neighbor assuming they were engaging in a tryst. Either way Walt was clearly nervous.

"Did you see anyone on your way over?" Walt asked. He closed the door firmly.

"No one. Not a sign of Abe at all. I'm not sure where Eddy is hiding, but he should be in position by now." Samantha looked towards the kitchen window. "I'm sure he and Jo aren't far."

"I hope not." Walt grimaced. "I have to be honest I'm a little bit nervous about all of this."

"Of course you are, Walt. We all are." She reached out and took his hand in hers to offer him some comfort. However, the moment she touched his hand he pulled his away, almost as if she had pinched him. "Sorry." She grimaced as she realized that she had probably taken him by surprise.

"Oh, it's okay, I'm the one that should be sorry. You were just being kind. I'm just a little jumpy, and it makes my anxious behavior go through the roof." He shook his head. "I have to make sure when I get like this that I concentrate and try to stay calm so my mind stays clear."

Samantha couldn't imagine Walt's mind ever not being clear. She considered him one of the most intelligent people that she had ever met. But she understood his concern.

"It's all going to be fine. Abe might not even show up," she lowered her voice. "What we think happened is still just a hunch until we can prove it."

"I know you're right, but to be honest I'm not sure if I'm more scared of him showing up or not showing up." Walt looked worried. "If he doesn't, then what will we do?"

"Then we'll regroup. Let's just try to stay focused on tonight. I think I should get in the closet now and stay hidden. You just go through your normal bedtime routine, that way if Abe is spying from somewhere, he won't think anything is amiss."

"All right, I made sure it was tidy for you, and there's a little dressing bench in there that you can sit on." Walt led her towards his bedroom. Samantha smiled at his accommodating behavior. While Walt might be a little stunted when it came to social behavior he certainly did know how to be a good friend.

Walt certainly had set up his closet nicely. But she didn't imagine it was too hard to do since everything was perfectly in place. His clothes were arranged according to color. His shoes were lined up very carefully, and although they all seemed to be the same color Walt appeared to have put them in a certain order. Even his ties were hung up by shape and color.

"Are you sure that you're going to be okay in here?" Walt asked with some concern. "I just worry that you'll get bored, or stiff, or what if you fall asleep?"

"I'll be fine." Samantha smiled at him. "I just had a cup of coffee and I am ready to spend a few hours with my thoughts."

"Okay." Walt nodded. He looked at her as if he might say more, then he turned away from the closet. "Just let me know if you need anything."

"Thank you, Walt. I think I have everything that I need."

Samantha reached out and closed the closet door. There were slats on it just wide enough that she could see movement through. She heard the sink in the bathroom as Walt brushed his teeth. Then she heard the creek of the bed as he sprawled out in it.

Samantha felt strange hidden away in his closet, as if she was spying on him. She knew that he had been feeling just as strange. As she waited for the minutes to pass by she did sink into her thoughts. She had been wondering if there was ever going to be an opportunity for her to write again. Of course she still wrote whenever she could, but she hadn't had an article published in a very long time. As she sorted through her thoughts time slowly passed.

***

Jo shifted her foot slightly. It had fallen asleep and she was trying to get the feeling back into it. In the past she had done plenty of stakeouts of places she wanted to break into, but it had been a while since she had endured such a long wait.

"Shh!" Eddy hissed at her. Her foot had rustled a few leaves.

"You shh," she shot back and glared at him.

They were hunched down in a thicket of trees with some underbrush. It was beside the corner of Walt's villa. It was just large enough to be called a wooded area, though it really was just a patch of trees. It provided a good amount of cover, especially in the dark so that they could keep a close eye on what was happening. They could see most of the back of the villa and the side of the villa where the bedroom window was. If Abe attempted to come in the front door, they might not see him, but Samantha knew to alert them the moment that she thought someone was inside.

"Listen, if you make too much noise you could scare him off," Eddy cautioned her with a scowl.

"If you keep talking about how much noise I'm making, you're definitely going to scare him off," Jo admonished. It had been two hours since they got into position. Jo was starting to think that Abe was not coming at all. Eddy however was just as vigilant as he had been in the first few minutes.

"You might think this is a joke, Jo, but I am responsible for the people inside that villa. If anyone gets hurt, it's going to be on me. So please, just stand still."

"I am standing still, Eddy. We all made the choice to be here, remember?" she softened her voice slightly. She knew that his nerves were likely on edge as he anticipated Abe's presence.

"It doesn't matter who made what choice, if someone gets hurt, it will be on me." Eddy stared at the villa. Jo could see the tension in his jaw. She could almost see what it must have been like for him to be in uniform. Because of her past Jo had always had an aversion to police officers, but now that she had the opportunity to get to know Eddy well, she could admire the bravery and backbone it took to wear a uniform and wield a gun. He didn't do it for any of the reasons that she suspected cops did. To her he did it because he wanted to help and to protect. There was definitely something admirable about that.

Jo was silent as she too watched the villa. The night had grown cold as the minutes ticked by. Although most of the residents were sound asleep there was still a lot of noise surrounding them. The water splashed with playful fish and insects. The leaves above them fluttered now and then in the subtle breeze. In the distance traffic on the highway could be heard. Jo was listening so closely that everything sounded much louder than she was used to.

"Do you think he's coming?" she spoke in a whisper.

"I hope so." Eddy's jaw rippled. "If he doesn't then we'll have a whole new set of problems."

"What if he didn't do it, Eddy?" Jo asked. "Everyone was so sure that Tommy did it, and it turned out not to be true. What if it wasn't Abe at all?" She studied him closely. Eddy did not look away from the villa and the grounds that surrounded it. He answered her under his breath.

"Someone will show up tonight. If it's not Abe, then it will be someone. We might have pinned it on the wrong person at first, but we figured that out. Abe is clever. I should have suspected him from the start, but I made too many assumptions. When he came up to me shortly after Joel died and asked me for my help, he threw me off his trail completely. He's been too careful about this whole thing. I know he's not going to risk Walt finding something in Joel's accounts that will point at him. Abe has to know that we'll find out that the payments were from him to Joel, and that will only lead to suspicion. The police will figure it out eventually, we just got down to it a little faster than they could."

"Still, it all seems a little outlandish to me." Jo crossed her arms as she stared at the back of the villa. "Why would someone go to such lengths? Just because Joel found out about Abe committing fraud? Sure, if Abe told the truth he would get in some trouble, but it wouldn't be the end of the world. It just doesn't seem like something that someone would kill for, you know?"

"It depends on what matters to you I guess." Eddy put a finger to his lips. He gestured to something beyond the villa on the walkway. As Jo looked she saw slow movement. At first it was just a shadow, then the figure moved under a streetlight. It was Abe in his wheelchair. As he rolled closer to the villa Jo could hear the grinding of his wheels against the pavement. It was the subtlest sound, but to her ears it was loud. Her heart began to pound. She realized for the first time that this was happening. There was no going back. Abe was going to break into Walt's house. Suddenly, Jo wondered if they had made a mistake.

"Should we stop him before he goes in?" Jo asked.

"Shh," Eddy instructed.

Jo glared at him. She was worried. Samantha and Walt were inside the villa like sitting ducks.

What if Abe decided not to take any chances this time? What if he had gotten a gun? She felt very anxious as Abe left the walkway and started along the driveway that led up to Walt's villa. There was a pathway that sprouted off the driveway and around the side of the house. For a moment neither Jo nor Eddy could see Abe as he was in front of the house.

Jo started to take a step forward to see where he was headed. She was worried that he would break in through the front. What if Samantha and Walt were sleeping? What if he was too quiet for them to hear him? She was almost out from the cover of the trees when Eddy grabbed her roughly around the waist. She gulped but did not cry out as he pulled her back. Her hands curled around his instinctively and tried to break his grasp. Eddy held her firmly with one arm and used his free hand to point to the corner of the house. Abe had just rounded the corner and was nearing the bedroom window.

"Stay still, don't blow this," Eddy hissed in Jo's

ear. Jo felt terrible as he released her. If she had stepped out like she intended to Abe would have seen her in a second. Their whole plan would have been ruined. But there wasn't time to dwell on that. She had to be ready to go as soon as Samantha gave the signal. She was going to be Eddy's back-up.

Eddy was so tense that she could see sweat building on his brow. His eyes were fixated on Abe. He watched as Abe wheeled the chair beneath the bedroom window. Still, there was a slight doubt within him that what he suspected could be true. However, in the next moment Abe looked all around to make sure no one was watching. Then he eased himself up into a standing position in the seat of the chair. Eddy was stunned by the sight. After seeing Abe for so long in his wheelchair, to see him standing was a lot to grasp. Abe peered through the bedroom window.

Chapter Seventeen

Inside the bedroom Walt stared hard at the wall. He had been staring at the same chip in the paint for quite some time. He was racking his brain for the name of the color of the paint. He would have to go first thing in the morning and buy the paint so that he could fix the chip. He would never sleep again if he didn't. He just hoped that the paint would be the same shade. Sometimes people claimed it was, but then it turned out that it wasn't. That was so frustrating. Really there was no excuse for it. Suddenly Walt felt fear grip his spine. He wasn't sure why until he saw the shadow on the wall. It was the shadow of a head in the window. It moved back and forth slowly.

Walt didn't dare to move a muscle. He was sure that it had to be Abe. If Abe saw him move then he might decide to call the whole thing off. It was hard not to move though, as Walt wanted to go running and screaming out of the villa. The very thought of someone watching him while he slept, even though he was just pretending, was beyond unsettling. He wondered if Samantha was okay in the closet. Was she still awake? Did she see the shadow on the wall? He didn't think that she could from her vantage point. He did his best not to squirm or scream as he watched the shadow on the wall. He held his breath for as long as he could.

Inside the closet Samantha was plotting a novel. She was fairly certain that she could pull it off in just a few weeks. She had already mentally created a colorful cast of characters, all of which had some kind of personal flaw that she found downright amusing. She was already writing the first chapter in her mind when she noticed that Walt's steady, regular breathing had stopped. In fact it didn't seem like he was breathing at all.

Samantha thought she might be mistaken and leaned closer to the closet door. She listened intently and waited for the sound to begin again. After a few moments she still didn't hear any type of breathing. Her mind began to spin with all of the explanations for this. Had Walt stopped breathing in his sleep? Had Abe already broken in and gotten to Walt without her realizing it? If only she had paid closer attention she might have known. She was nearly in a panic as she reached for the doorknob. If Walt needed help she had to get out there and help him, it didn't matter what risk she might be taking. Just when she was about to turn the knob on the closet door she heard Walt sigh. It was a soft, slow sound, but it was a sound of life that she needed to hear. She lowered her hand from the doorknob. She was relieved that she hadn't rushed out and made a fool of herself. She was sure that Walt would not have appreciated that.

Samantha checked the time on her phone. It was well after midnight. She wondered just how long they were going to wait for Abe to show up. She yawned and leaned her head against the back of the closet. She needed to be able to stay awake, so her thoughts returned to the first chapter of her novel. As she considered it, she decided the whole thing was garbage, tossed out the idea, and started all over again.

***

"What is he doing?" Jo whispered to Eddy. Eddy had expected Abe to open the bedroom window and climb in. Instead he sat back down in his wheelchair.

"He was checking to see that Walt was inside. He wanted to make sure that he was asleep. He's not going in that way." Eddy narrowed his eyes as Abe began to roll along the back of the house.

The living room window was fully accessible with no brush or bushes to get in his way. He rolled right up to it. Eddy reached out and held Jo's elbow. It was partially to restrain her, and partially to comfort her. Watching a murderer break into their friend's home was not exactly the best feeling in the world.

As Abe got to his feet in the seat of the

wheelchair again it was clear that this time he was going to make his entrance. He slowly raised the window. Eddy had to bite into his bottom lip to stop himself from bolting after him. He knew that Abe had to get inside. They had to trap him, or all of this would prove nothing. Jo looked over at him anxiously. Eddy held up his free hand to warn her not to move just yet. Eddy's stomach twisted with repulsion as he watched Abe's lithe frame disappear through the living room window. Abe was now inside Walt's villa. His empty wheelchair was waiting for his return.

"Now?" Jo pleaded.

"Not just yet." Eddy looked into her eyes. "Trust me."

Jo scowled at him. She didn't feel the need to trust him, when he obviously didn't offer her the same. Still, she waited as he requested. Her heart was pounding. She wondered if Walt and Samantha were aware that Abe was inside.

***

Walt thought he heard something, but he told himself it was nothing. He had to, or he might scream. Samantha was in the closet, she would witness everything if he were to freak out. He had often been told by women that he was not manly enough. He had taken that to heart. He knew that his cleanliness and obsession with detail was hard enough to deal with. Samantha was his friend, but even she would likely laugh at him if he panicked and ran for the door.

So, he remained still and pretended that he had not heard what he thought was the living room window opening. He could only hope that Eddy had seen the figure in the window. Eddy had promised he would keep an eye on the situation and intervene when the time was right. But what if he had fallen asleep? What if he had given up and already gone home? What if he was distracted by Jo? Walt squeezed his eyes shut. Just be calm, he pleaded with himself.

Samantha heard rummaging in the living room. It was quiet, but distinct enough that she knew what it was. She heard papers sliding against papers, and drawers slowly opening and closing. There was no question in her mind that someone was searching the living room. Abe had come after all. She stood up to prepare herself to protect Walt if she needed to. She pulled out her phone and sent a quick text to Eddy.

Abe is in the house.

She knew that Eddy wouldn't text back. They had agreed it wasn't worth the risk unless it was an emergency. As Samantha peered through the slats in the closet door she waited for Abe to show his face. Would he come into the bedroom? Would Eddy confront him in the living room? She wasn't sure what would happen next. As she thought about this it occurred to her that everyone who was gathered at the memorial had overheard what Eddy had said. If the killer wasn't Abe, it might be someone else entirely in the living room. In that case she really had no idea what to expect. The rummaging continued. Samantha noticed that Walt had shifted slightly in the bed. She still couldn't tell if he was awake or not. She was tempted to try to whisper to him, but she was afraid it would draw attention to the bedroom.

After what seemed like hours, but was likely only a minute or two, Samantha heard footsteps in the hallway leading towards the bedroom. Her heart lurched. She wondered if he would head straight for the closet. It really was the only place to hide in the bedroom, so it would be the first place a criminal would check to make sure no one else was in the house. If he did, she might be spotted before anyone had the chance to stop him. Would he be armed? Would he be angry enough to harm Walt or her?

Chapter Eighteen

Samantha held her breath as she saw a flicker of light across the carpet. Through the slats of the closet door she saw a figure walking gingerly through the bedroom. She knew what happened next in the plan, but her heart was still pounding. Suddenly, the light in the bedroom turned on and flooded the room. The figure froze. Before he could react, Walt jumped up from the bed. He tossed his blanket over the head of the figure and tackled him at the same time. Both went crashing to the floor. Samantha opened the door to the closet and headed straight to the window. She opened it, and Eddy climbed in. Walt was still struggling with whoever was under the blanket on the floor. Eddy charged over to them and tore off the blanket.

Abe lay on the floor with his eyes wide open. He froze at the sight of everyone staring down at him.

"Abe, it must be a miracle." Eddy glowered down at him. "Or you're a murderous con artist."

Abe jumped to his feet and lunged for the door. Eddy tackled him before he could reach it. Abe thrashed and tried to wriggle his way out from under Eddy. Eddy kept him pinned down with the full force of his weight and his training.

"Get off me!" Abe exclaimed. "Are you people crazy?"

"We're the crazy ones?" Samantha laughed. "We're not the ones who have been faking the need for a wheelchair for many years. We're not the ones who broke into a neighbor's house, and we are certainly not the ones who murdered Joel Westons."

"You don't know what you're talking about!" Abe growled and bucked upward in an attempt to shake Eddy off his back. Eddy easily kept him under control.

"We have everything recorded, Abe!" Eddy pointed to the camera in the corner of Walt's room. "Try explaining to the police that you just happened to be in Walt's house, without your wheelchair. What were you looking for?" Eddy slowly eased to his feet. He remained close enough to grab Abe again if he needed to. "The ledger?"

Abe stood up slowly. He eyed Eddy who had one hand tightly gripping his arm. "Why do you think?" he asked sarcastically. "Of course the ledger. I wasn't going to let anyone find out the truth."

"Is that why you killed Joel?" Samantha asked quietly. "Because you were afraid he was going to expose you?"

"Afraid? No! I knew he was going to expose me. He set up cameras everywhere to try to catch me. He thought because I didn't seem to be depressed about my condition that I couldn't possibly not be able to walk. He accused me more than once, but he never had any proof. I was always so careful."

"So, how did he catch you?" Walt asked. His eyes narrowed with genuine interest. Abe had them all fooled for so long, he wanted to know how it was that Joel had figured out something that no one else had. How had Abe slipped up? Had Joel found out with his own set up?

"I made one mistake." Abe frowned. "When I started all of this I promised myself that no matter what I did I would never get out of the chair. As long as I didn't get out of the chair, no one could catch me. I even moved myself from the chair to the toilet and into the shower using all of the assistance products I had purchased."

"So then how?" Samantha pressed.

Abe lowered his gaze to his hands. "You'd probably have to ask Anna about that."

"What? What could Anna possibly have to do with any of this?" Eddy asked. "Don't you try to spin another one of your cons, Abe!" He was already on the edge of fury and Abe's excuses were pushing him even closer.

Abe sighed. He closed his eyes briefly, then opened them again. "The thing is, Joel never really took care of Anna. You know, he made sure that she had everything that she needed financially, but as far as emotionally, and intimately, he was never there for her. I always thought she was a looker. So, when Joel offered me the opportunity to invest in a new business, I decided to go for it. I had a little money to spare, and I always wanted more. Plus, it would give me the chance to get to know Anna a little better."

"Then when the business tanked?" Walt pressed. He had seen people do desperate things over the loss of money, but nothing so terrible.

"I figured out what Joel was up to. I mean, a con artist always knows another con artist. I wanted my money back. I decided to go to Anna and tell her what a crook she was married to. Well, Anna and I got to talking. We ended up spending more and more time together. Joel refused to give me back my money. I hated the fact that Anna was married to such a jerk."

"You two fell in love?" Samantha asked incredulously. "Is it even possible for a man like you to love someone?"

"Hey, I'm still a person." Abe glared at her. "Just because my career choice doesn't suit you, that doesn't make me any less of a person. I'm human. I have feelings. She acted like I was her one true love." He rolled his eyes and shook his head. "I may be a talented con artist, but I'm still capable of being an idiot."

"Maybe, but I just wouldn't expect someone like you to have such strong emotions about anyone or anything." Samantha frowned and looked towards Eddy. "Maybe we should call in the police."

"Do what you want. It doesn't matter now." Abe hung his head with clear shame and embarrassment. "I did fall in love. I didn't think I was capable of it, but Anna was so kind. She always helped me with anything I needed. She was always concerned about my medications. She stood up for me if anyone gave me a hard time." His eyes narrowed sharply. "I was such a fool!"

"What did you do, Abe?" Eddy asked, his voice edged with frustration. He wanted the truth.

Abe bit into his bottom lip as if he wanted to hold the confession inside. But there was a sadness in his eyes that made it clear he just wanted to finally get it out. He wanted to be free of the burden that he was carrying.

"Anna and I were getting closer and closer. It was such an intimate romance. I couldn't imagine my life without her. I wanted her to leave Joel and marry me. But I didn't think she would, because even though she was so kind, what woman would really want to commit to spending the rest of her life taking care of someone in a wheelchair?" He shrugged. "So, I made the stupidest mistake I ever could have. I told her the truth, about everything."

"You did?" Walt asked with surprise. "That was a huge risk to take." Eddy and Samantha looked at Abe with surprise as well.

Jo stepped in through the bedroom door. "Everyone okay in here?" she asked.

"We're fine." Samantha nodded.

"I know it was stupid." Abe shook his head. "At first she claimed that she didn't believe me. So, I proved it to her. I stood up, and I hugged her." He closed his eyes at the memory. "It felt so good to finally hold her."

Eddy frowned with some sympathy in his expression. "What did she do when you proved it to her?"

"What did she do?" Abe raised his voice. "She took a video is what she did! She had been playing me the whole time. As soon as Joel found out that I knew about his shady scams, that I knew what he was doing with the money that he was supposed to be investing, he made her try to gain my trust. I was furious. She told me there was nothing she could do."

"That's when you started paying Joel to keep

your secret?" Walt asked.

"Yes." Abe scowled.

"But that wasn't enough was it? You were always worried that Joel would come out with the truth?" Eddy tightened his grasp on Abe's arm.

"It wasn't even that," Abe admitted quietly. "It might make more sense if it was."

"Then what was it?" Samantha asked. "Why did you have to kill him? He might have been a con artist, too, but he was still a person, Abe. You murdered him! All because of money?"

"No!" Abe had tears in his eyes as he looked at Samantha. "It wasn't because of the money. I would have happily paid him for the rest of my life. He had pulled the wool over my eyes, he won, there is honor among con artists."

"Then why did you kill him?" Walt asked with confusion.

"It was because of her," Abe whispered. "She was everything to me. She told me that he was the reason we couldn't be together, that he had forced her to get the video of me standing up. She told me that she was afraid of him, and that she couldn't leave him because she wasn't sure what he would do. She said that she wished he was gone. She had me believing that she loved me and would be with me, even if I had nothing. So, it just felt like Joel was standing between me and the love of my life."

"So, you killed him to protect Anna?" Samantha said with a hint of sadness in her voice. It was no excuse to kill a man, but it made a little more sense to her than murdering over money.

"I thought I did," Abe muttered and looked away shamefully. "I thought it would be worth it. I kept losing my courage, but when I saw the candlesticks through the window I knew what I had to do, I just went for it. I thought the world would be a better place without him anyway."

"And?" Eddy stared at him.

"And, she never loved me at all. As soon as Joel was dead she wanted nothing to do with me.

She threatened to expose my secret and the video if I told anyone the truth. She has been playing the act of a grieving widow ever since. Yes, I was the one who killed Joel, it was my hands, but Anna, she also wanted him dead." He drew his lips into a thin, flat line.

"Wow." Samantha shook her head. "You must have really loved her."

"Oh, please don't tell me that you're buying this, Sam?" Walt asked sternly.

"What do you mean?" Samantha frowned and looked between Abe and Walt.

"I mean this man is a professional con artist. We're supposed to believe he was in love? It sounds to me like he's just trying to take Anna down with him. There's no proof that she had anything to do with this." Walt shook his head. "I don't believe a single word that comes out of your mouth, Abe. Eddy, let's get the police."

Eddy nodded and pulled out his cell phone. He dialed one of his contacts at the department and requested that a patrol car come out.

"That's my cue to leave." Jo slipped past her friends towards the door. "Let me know what happens in the morning!"

"It is the morning." Walt smiled briefly at her as she walked past him.

"You know what I mean, Walt," Jo said with a hint of frustration.

"Don't you want to give a statement to the police?" Eddy asked.

"No thanks!" Jo waved her hand in the air without looking back. She made her way out through the front door of the villa. Abe was silent but Eddy knew better than to get lulled into a sense of comfort. Abe was smart enough and desperate enough to attempt an escape. Samantha was keeping an eye on him, too, but for a different reason. She was genuinely curious about his story. She prided herself on being someone who knew how to read people. The stricken expression on Abe's face made her think he might just be telling the truth. She moved slightly closer to him.

"Is Walt right, Abe? Did you really make all of that up about being in love?" She scrutinized his reaction.

Abe lifted his gaze to hers. His eyes were watering, perhaps with tears, or perhaps because of the rough way that Eddy had handled him.

"I did what I thought was right. I did what I thought I had to do," Abe's voice trembled a little as he spoke. "No one will ever believe me. But Anna will know the truth. Just ask yourself, Samantha, who gets the money in the end? Who gets everything?" He looked into her eyes with a sense of defeat and wonder.

To Samantha it seemed that he was more shocked than anyone else that Anna had been able to pull off such a clever and ruthless ruse. Samantha continued to stare at him with restrained fascination. She knew that with no one else to inherit his money, all of Joel's fortune would go to Anna. She had been stuck in a loveless marriage. Could she really have been cunning enough to con a con man into killing her husband so that she could be rid of him, but still have all of his money?

"You really believe she planned this whole thing, Abe?"

"If the money goes to her before the lawsuits are settled then those people who are suing Joel's company will not see a dime," Walt suddenly announced. "It's actually quite brilliant."

"What he said." Abe nodded as he glanced in Walt's direction. "The woman is more devious than anyone I have ever met."

"Don't listen to him," Eddy warned Samantha. "He's just trying to muddle the truth so that he has a chance in court."

"I can't believe that you think we should just let this go." Samantha looked in Eddy's direction. "Don't you think that justice should be served?"

"I think that you need to realize that there is a

difference between justice and what is actually possible. If Anna is responsible for orchestrating Joel's death, of course she should face some criminal charges. But what are the chances of being able to prove that? Do you think she wrote it down somewhere? It's her word against Abe's, and Abe just got outed as one of the most repulsive men to walk the face of the Earth. Who is going to believe his story over a grieving widow who has never had a mark on her record?" Eddy argued, though it was clear from the way he spoke that he was aggravated. Samantha was aggravated as well.

"But, that doesn't mean she can just get away with it." Samantha was getting more and more flustered by the minute. She was sure that Eddy couldn't seriously be suggesting that they just let Anna get away with it.

"It doesn't mean that she should." Eddy locked eyes with her. "But that doesn't change the fact that she most likely will." He looked at her apologetically. "Abe will give his statement I'm sure. The police will do what they can with it."

Before Samantha could reply the police burst through the door.

"Hands in the air!" The lead officer pointed his weapon at the entire group. Eddy raised his hands, followed by Walt, and Samantha. Abe raised his as well. His shoulders slumped as the officer walked up to him. He looked so resigned to his fate. Or perhaps he was just weighed down by heartbreak.

Chapter Nineteen

As Eddy explained the situation to the arresting officers, Abe was cuffed and led from the villa. Walt walked over to Samantha.

"Do you think they will believe Abe's story?" Walt asked.

"I don't know," Samantha said feeling confused. "I doubt it. He's told one too many lies to be believed now."

"Excuse me, Sir." One of the officers gestured to Walt. "I need you to file the report for the break in."

"Of course," Walt agreed. He glanced over at Samantha. "Are you okay?"

"Sure."

While Walt was speaking to one of the officers another came over to take Samantha's statement. She told the officer the entire tale from the plan to her suspicion of Anna's involvement. The officer's eyes glazed over about halfway through, but that might have been because of how fast Samantha was talking.

"Maybe I should write it out for you?" Samantha offered.

"Thanks, but I don't think that's necessary," the officer replied. "I think I got the most important details."

When the officer walked away from her Samantha slipped out of the bedroom and through the living room to the front door. She wanted to see them take Abe away. The more she thought about how he had betrayed not only his friend, but also his entire community the more it bothered her. Eddy followed her outside and stopped beside her on the front porch.

"What are we going to do about Anna?" Samantha asked. Eddy looked over at her with some apprehension.

"What do you mean what are we going to do about her?" He settled his gaze on Samantha.

"I mean we can't just let her get away with this," Samantha stated firmly as she looked towards the police car that was driving away with Abe in the backseat.

"Get away with what?" Eddy shrugged. "We have no idea if anything Abe said was true. He could have just been spinning a story in the hopes that he would get less jail time."

"Or he could have been telling the truth!"

"He could have been." Eddy nodded thoughtfully. "I'll see what I can do."

"Thanks," Samantha said with appreciation.

"I'll let you know if I find anything," he said. "But I don't like my chances. I promise I'll tell you if I find anything, you just make sure you get some rest."

"All right. You make sure you do, too."

"I will," he agreed.

Eddy's watched as Samantha walked away. His muscles were still tense from attacking Abe. When he had seen Abe in Walt's bedroom, his protective instincts had gone through the roof. He hated the idea that Abe might have hurt his friends. It was not something he could let go of easily.

Once Samantha had turned towards her villa Eddy stepped back inside to check on Walt.

"Are you doing okay?" Eddy asked him. Walt sat down on the easy chair in his living room and stared. He looked dazed.

"I think so. I have to say that's the closest I've ever come to a home invasion and I hope I never experience it again." He scowled. "I thought it would be fine since we all planned for it to happen, but it really wasn't."

"It's violating." Eddy nodded. "I know the feeling. But it will ease with a little time. The important thing is that nobody got hurt."

"Yes, you're right," Walt agreed with relief.

"Do you want to come to my place until the officers finish up?" Eddy offered. "You could catch a nap."

"No, that's okay. I'll wait until they're done. There's going to be a lot of straightening up to do." He gulped as one of the officers accidentally knocked over a carefully organized stack of magazines.

"All right then, I'm going to head out. Just let me know if there's anything that you need." He shook Walt's hand. "You did a great job."

Walt smiled in return. Then his gaze shifted back to the disarray that was occupying his mind.

Chapter Twenty

Samantha couldn't just sit in her villa. She had tried to sleep for hours, but found it impossible. Her mind kept returning to the thought of Abe sitting in his wheelchair, watching Joel and Anna's house. He had given up everything in his life for the con. He had made sure that he never made a mistake. All of the freedoms that most people took for granted, he gave up willingly, because he wanted money.

Early the next morning she decided to go for a walk by the lake to try and relax.

As she neared the lake Eddy walked towards her. "How are you doing, Sam?"

"I honestly don't know," Samantha said hesitantly. "There have been many times that I've researched crimes that went unpunished, but this is the first time I personally know someone is getting away with murder, and there is nothing I can do about it."

"Anna didn't actually kill him," Eddy pointed out. "That was all Abe's decision."

"I know," she said thoughtfully. "But she did have an influence on his decision. Anyway, it doesn't matter now, does it?" she added as she shook her head. "She's gotten away with it, and there's nothing that we can do about that."

"Oh, there might be a little something that can be done." Eddy raised an eyebrow with a mischievous smirk.

"What do you mean?" Samantha asked with surprise.

"Well, that's why I came to see you. I got a call from Chris and he found out that from what Abe told the police they have decided to further investigate Anna's involvement in the murder. Of course it will depend on what they can dig up, but trust me, Anna's luck is going to run out, and soon." He reached up and tipped his fedora slightly forward on his head. "There is no perfect crime, Samantha, at least not when we're around."

Samantha smiled at him. As they walked back down the hill towards the water, the tall grass swayed slowly as if beckoning to them. The familiar sound of the birds chirping and the glistening, blue lake made her feel at peace. Samantha felt that Sage Gardens was safe once again. She had never felt more at home.

The End

More Cozy Mysteries by Cindy Bell

Sage Gardens Cozy Mysteries
Birthdays Can Be Deadly

Money Can Be Deadly

Dune House Cozy Mysteries
Seaside Secrets

Boats and Bad Guys

Treasured History

Hidden Hideaways

Dodgy Dealings

Wendy the Wedding Planner Cozy Mysteries
Matrimony, Money and Murder

Chefs, Ceremonies and Crimes

Knives and Nuptials

Mice, Marriage and Murder

Heavenly Highland Inn Cozy Mysteries

Murdering the Roses

Dead in the Daisies

Killing the Carnations

Drowning the Daffodils

Suffocating the Sunflowers

Books, Bullets and Blooms

A Deadly serious Gardening Contest

A Bridal Bouquet and a Body

79836745R00137

Made in the USA
Middletown, DE
12 July 2018